AF261199

Am I Lost

The content of this work is 100% author-created,
not generated by Artificial Intelligence.

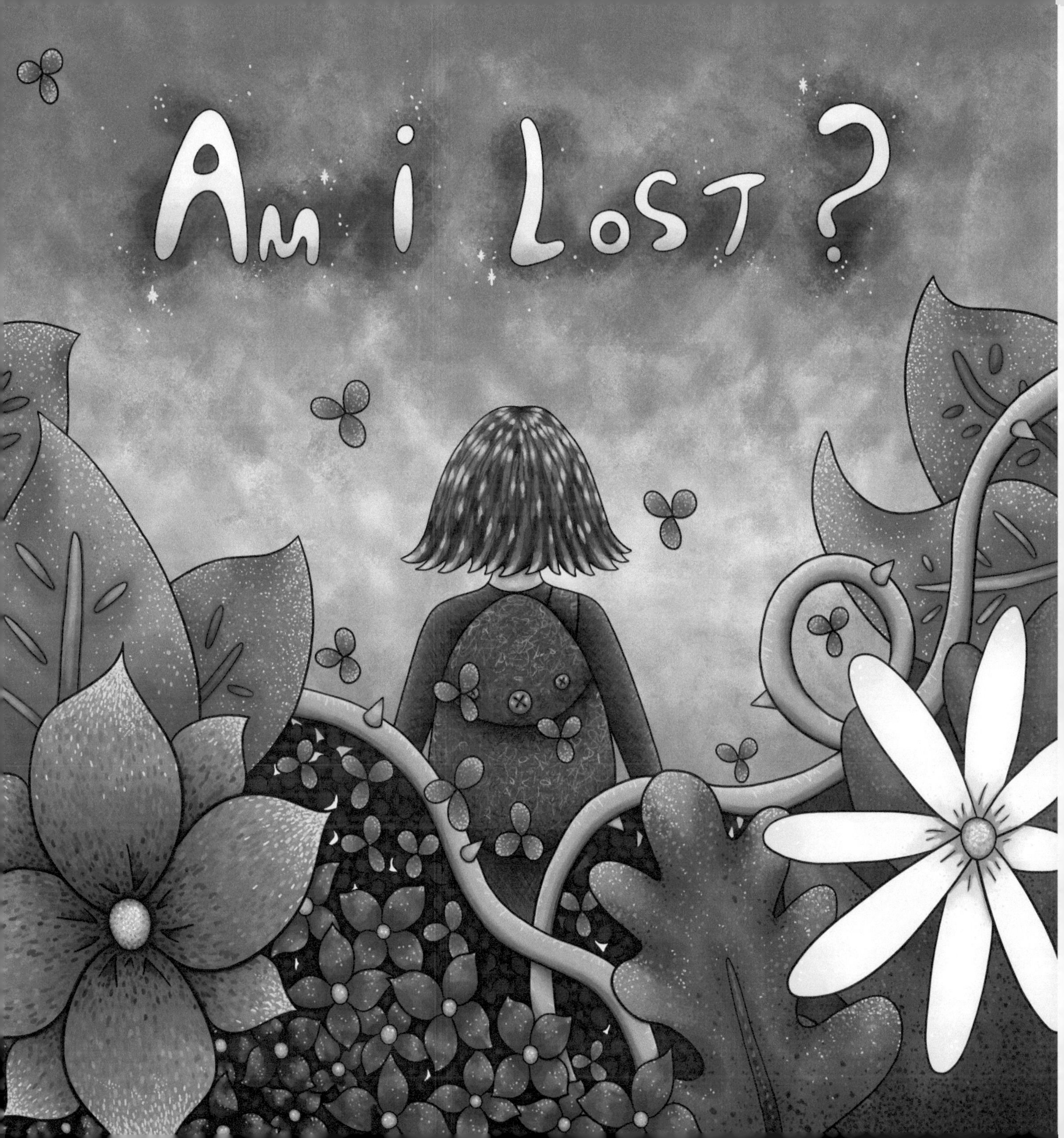

Am I Lost?

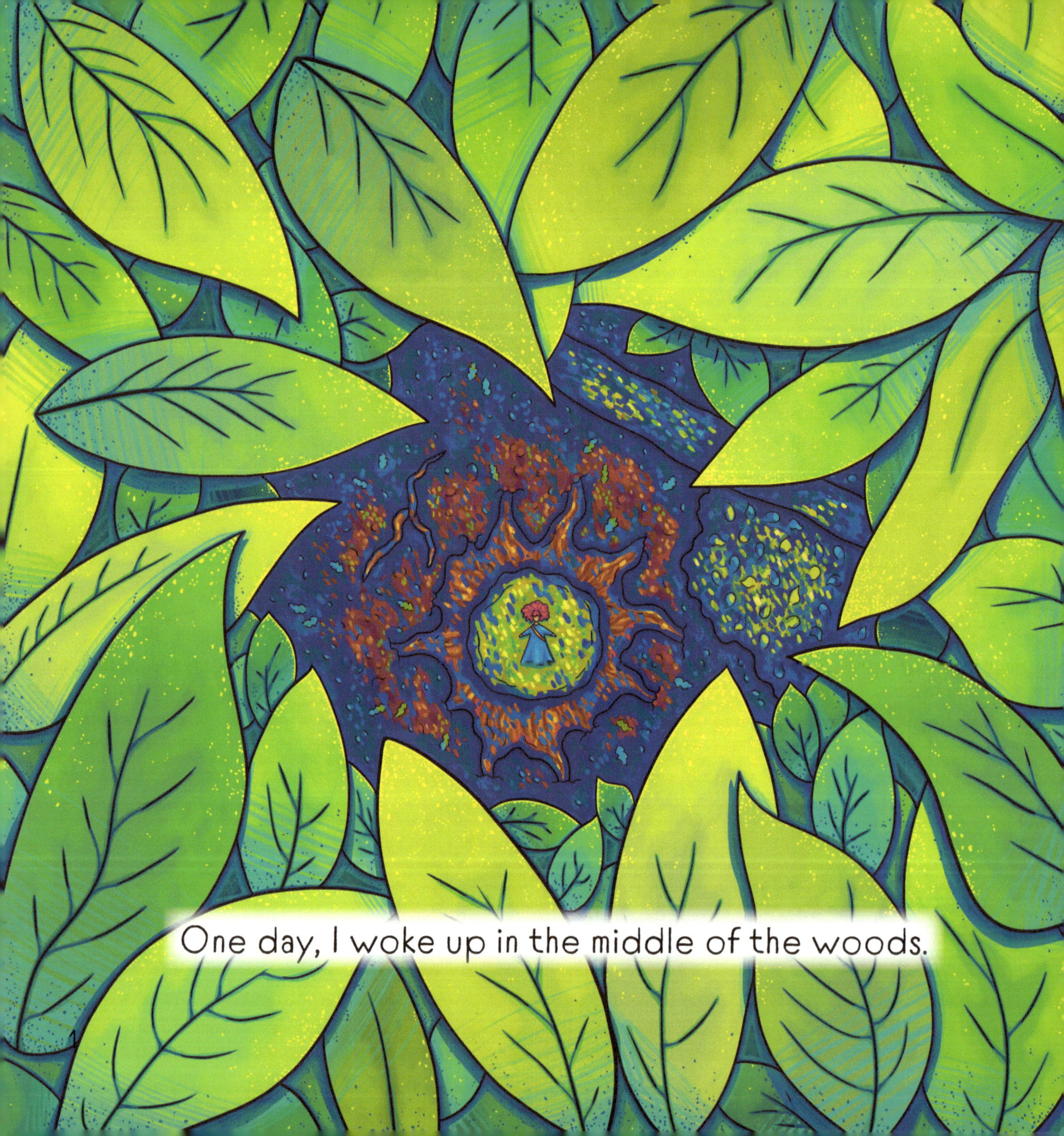

One day, I woke up in the middle of the woods.

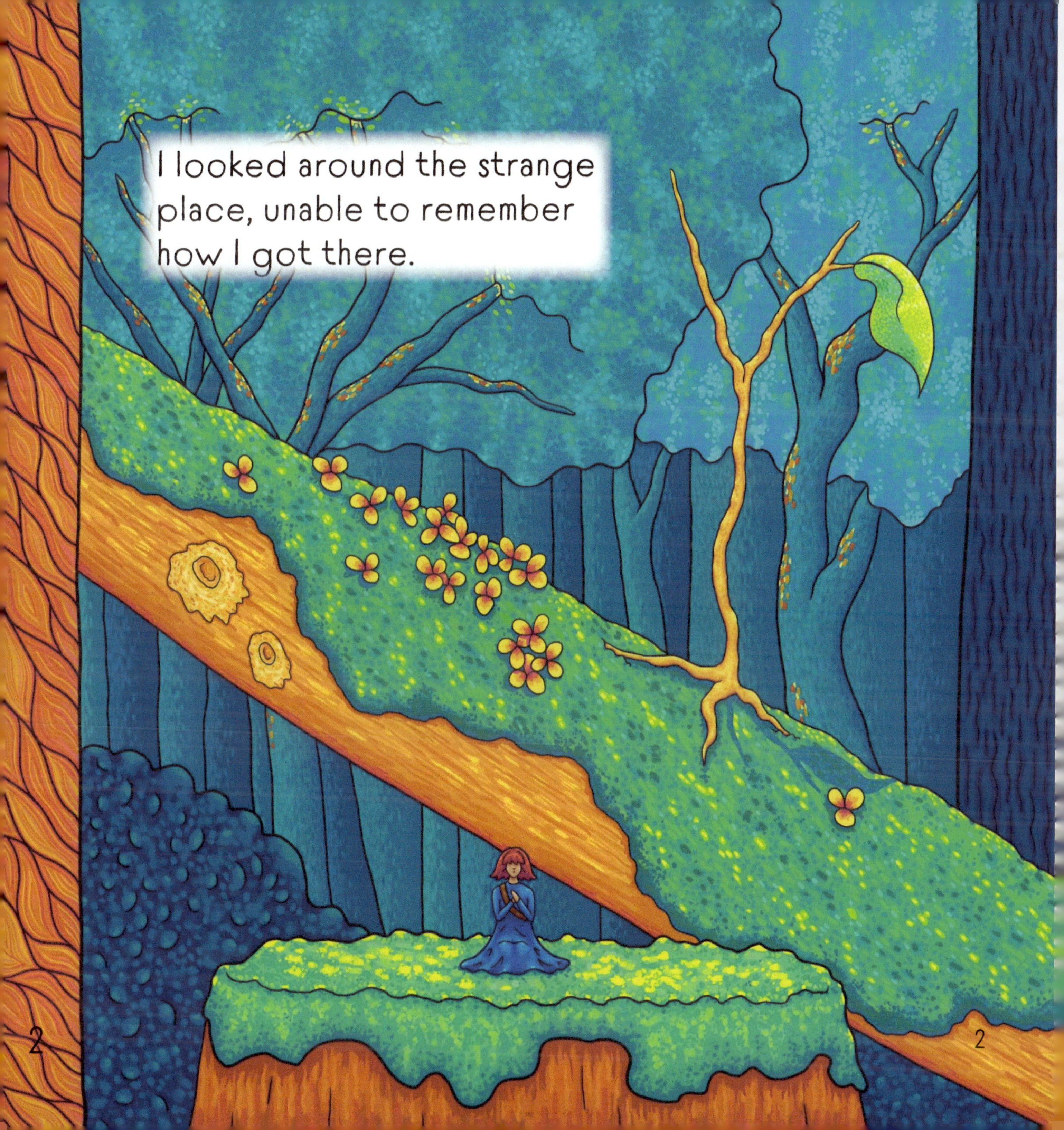

I looked around the strange place, unable to remember how I got there.

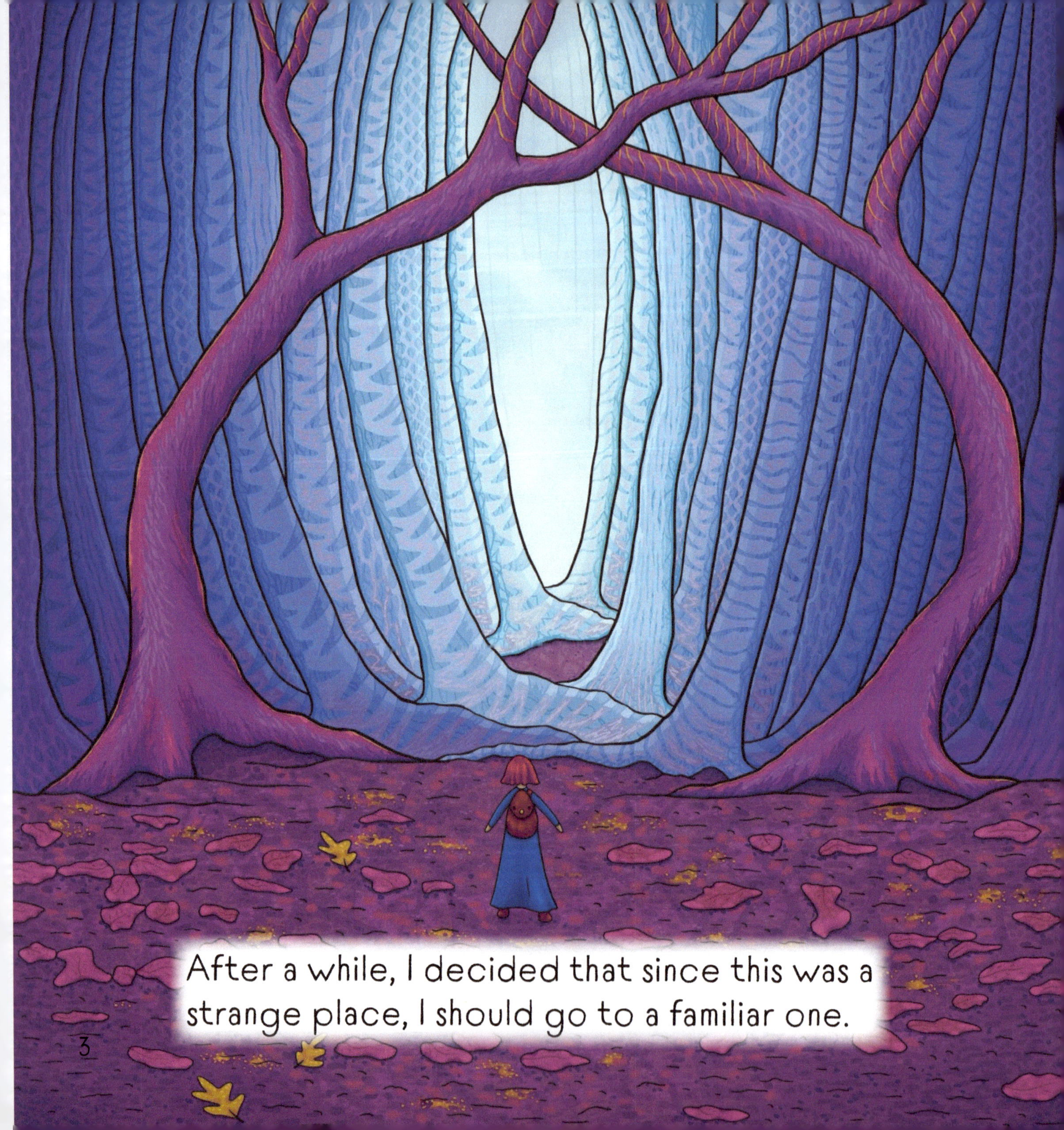
After a while, I decided that since this was a strange place, I should go to a familiar one.

3

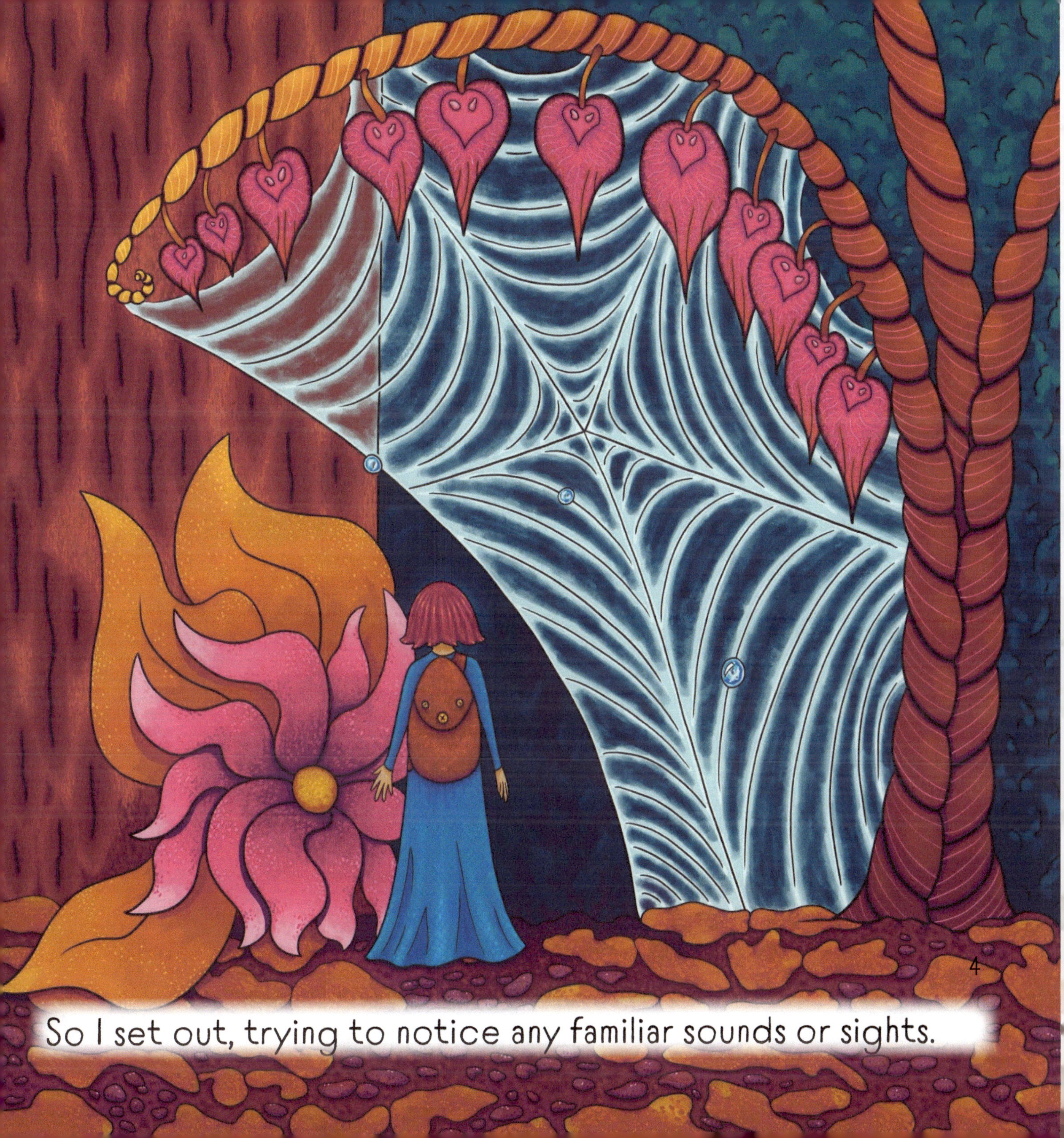

So I set out, trying to notice any familiar sounds or sights.

4

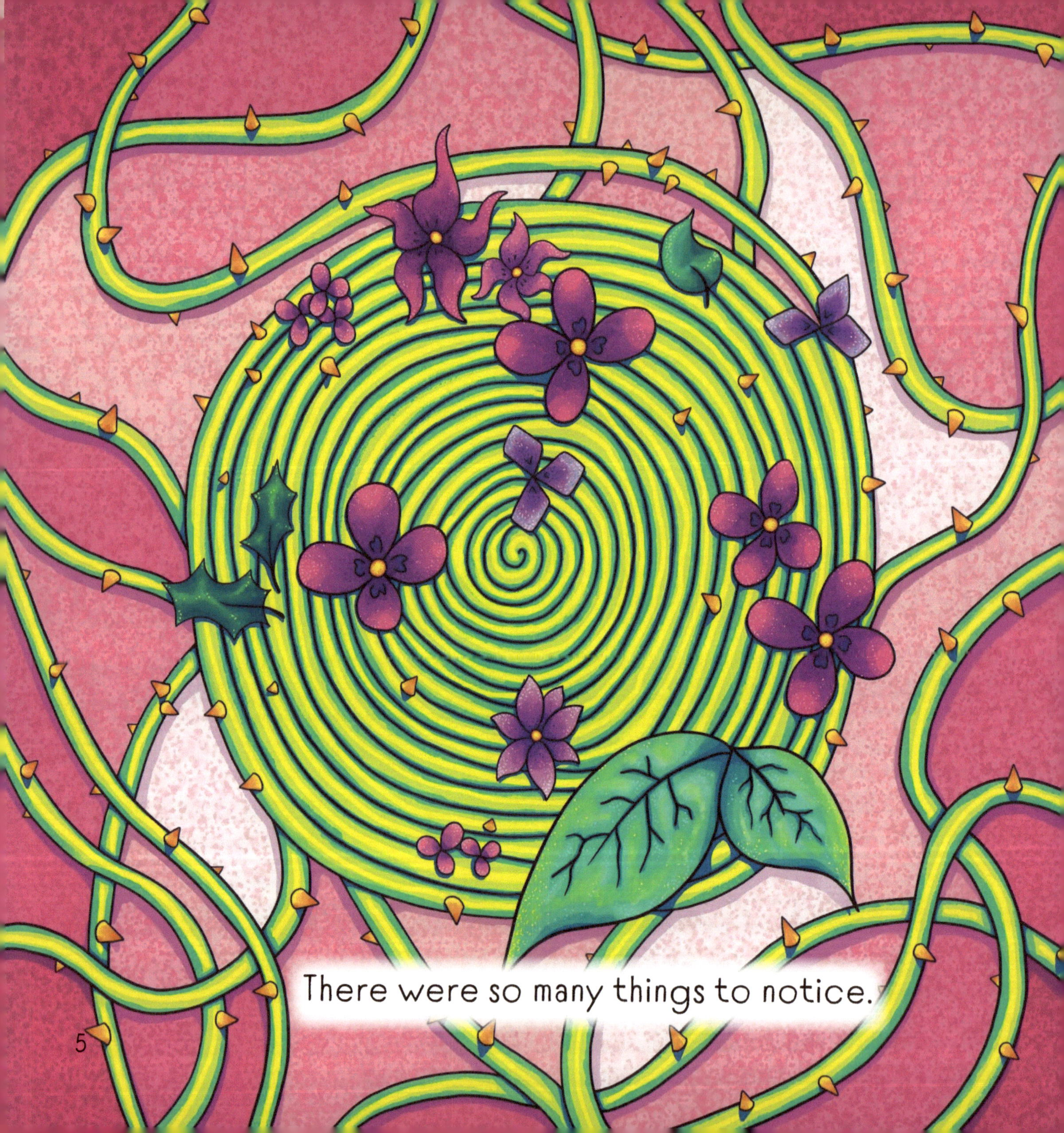

5

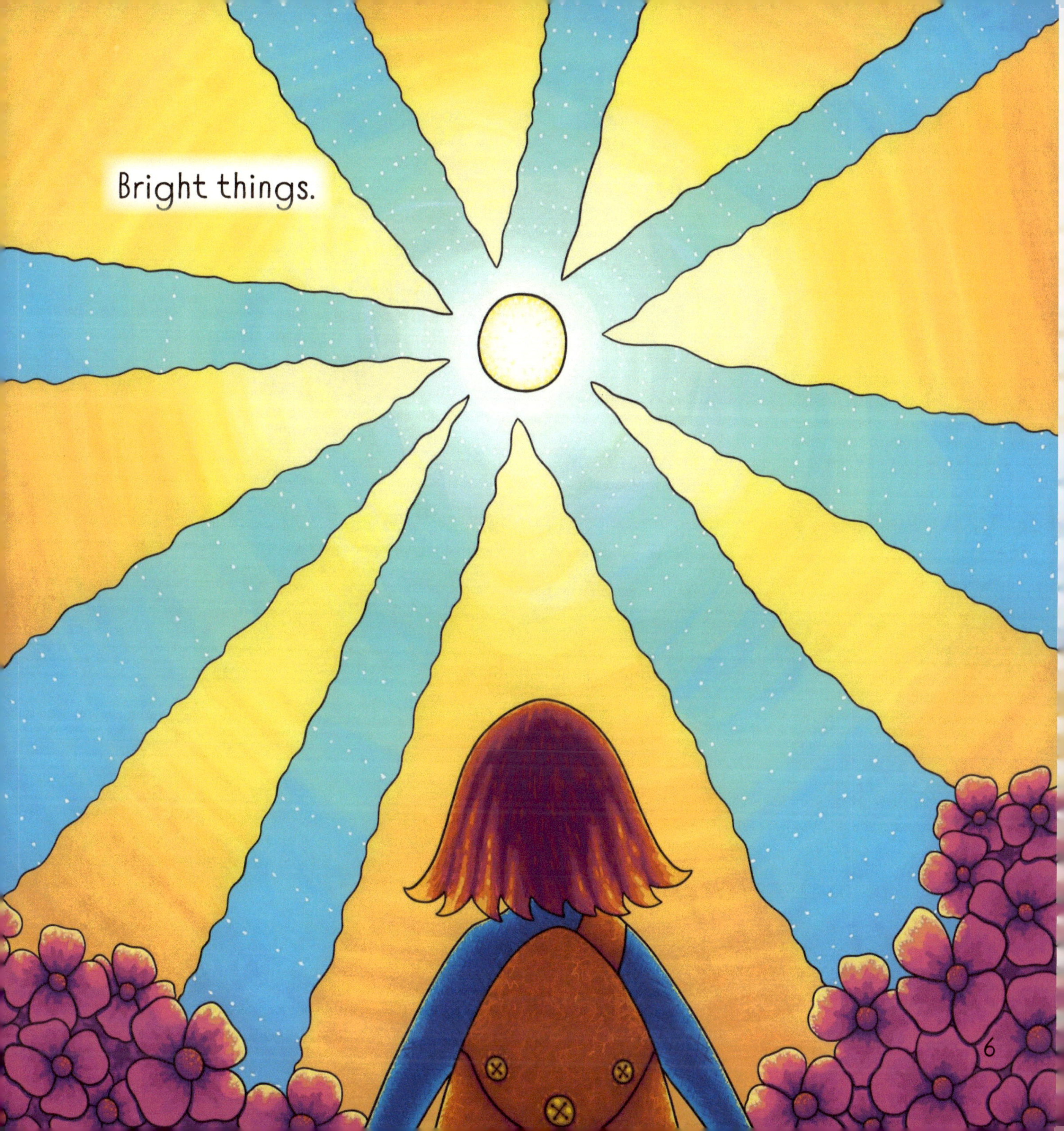
Bright things.

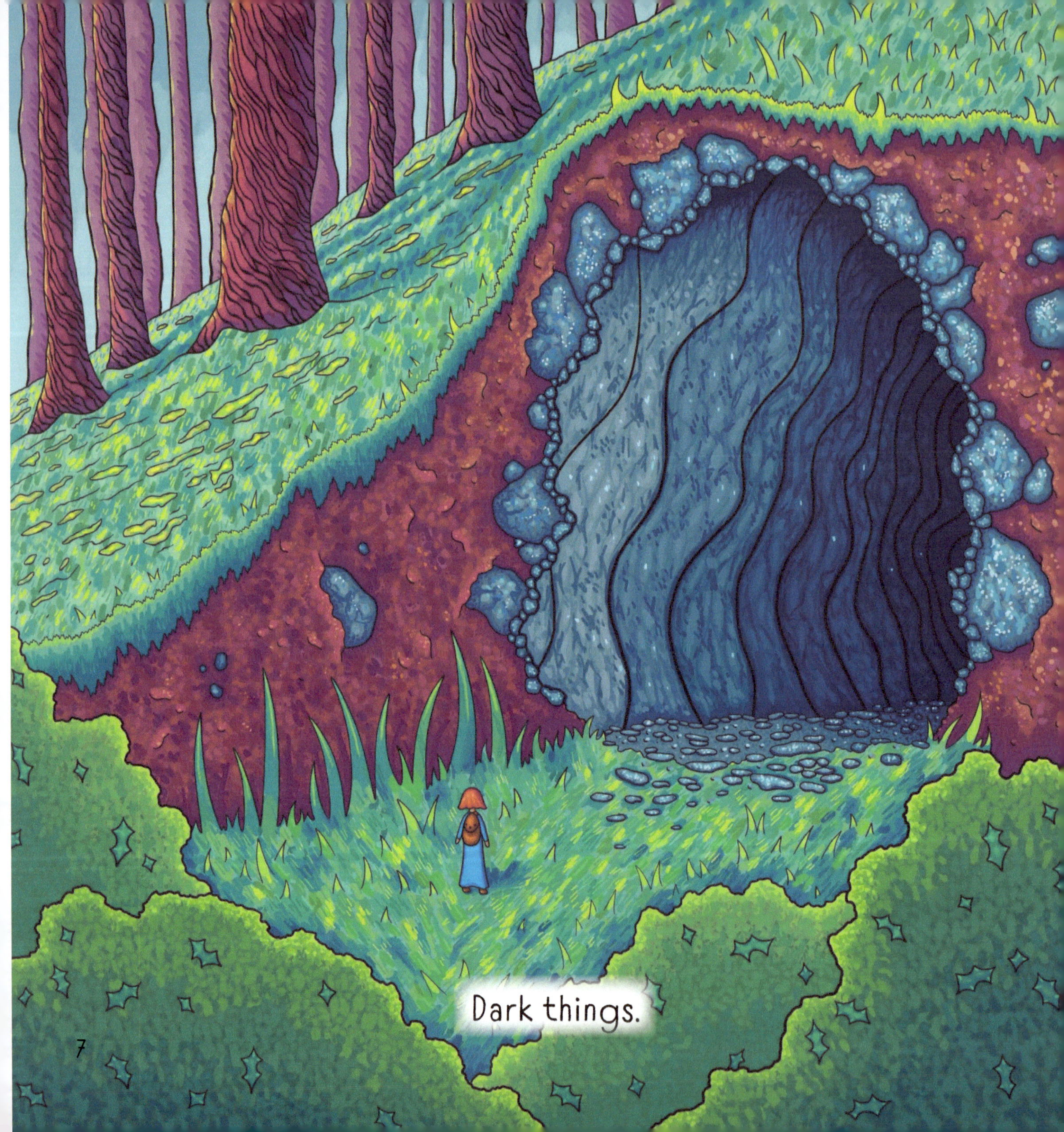

7

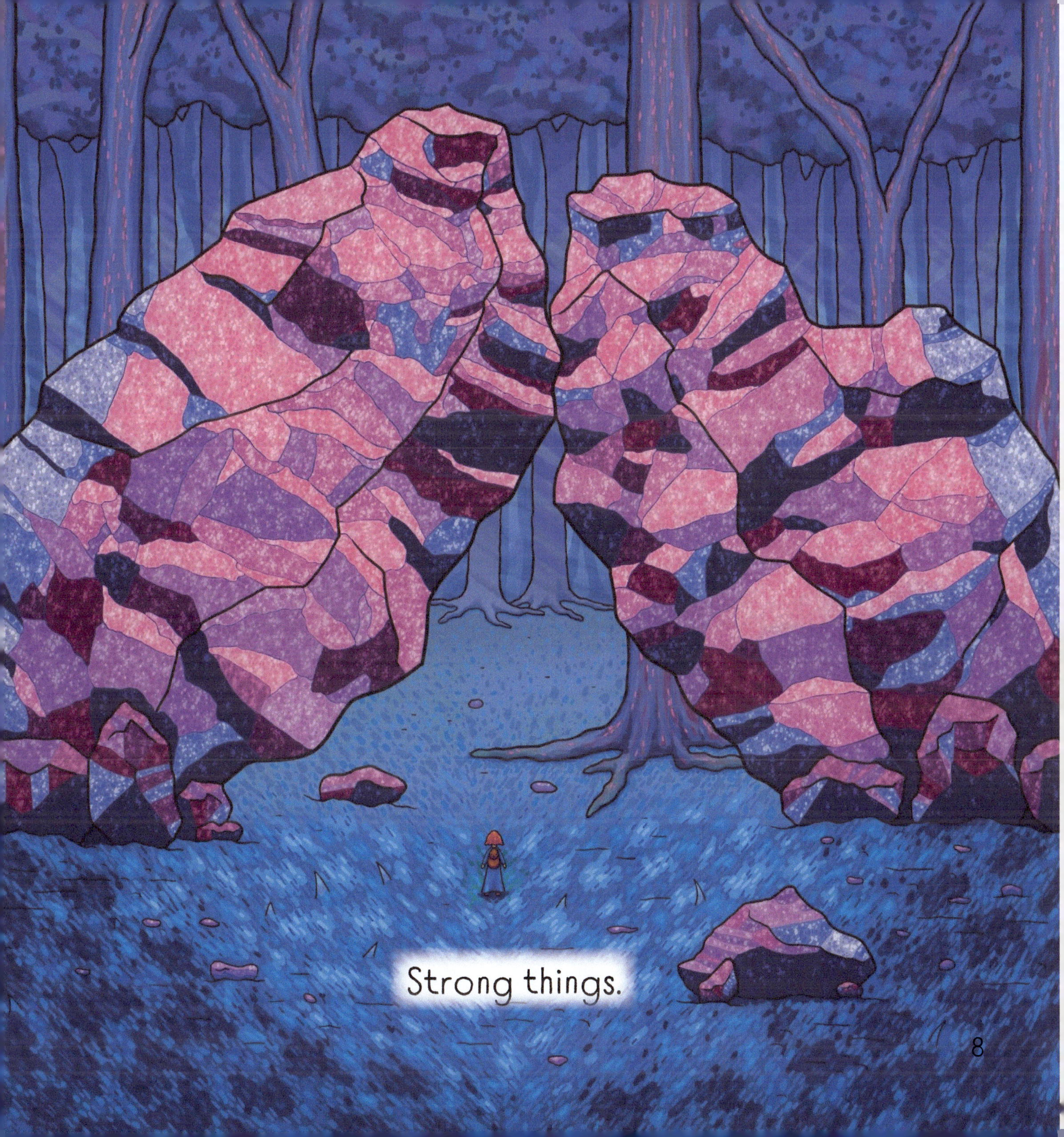
Strong things.

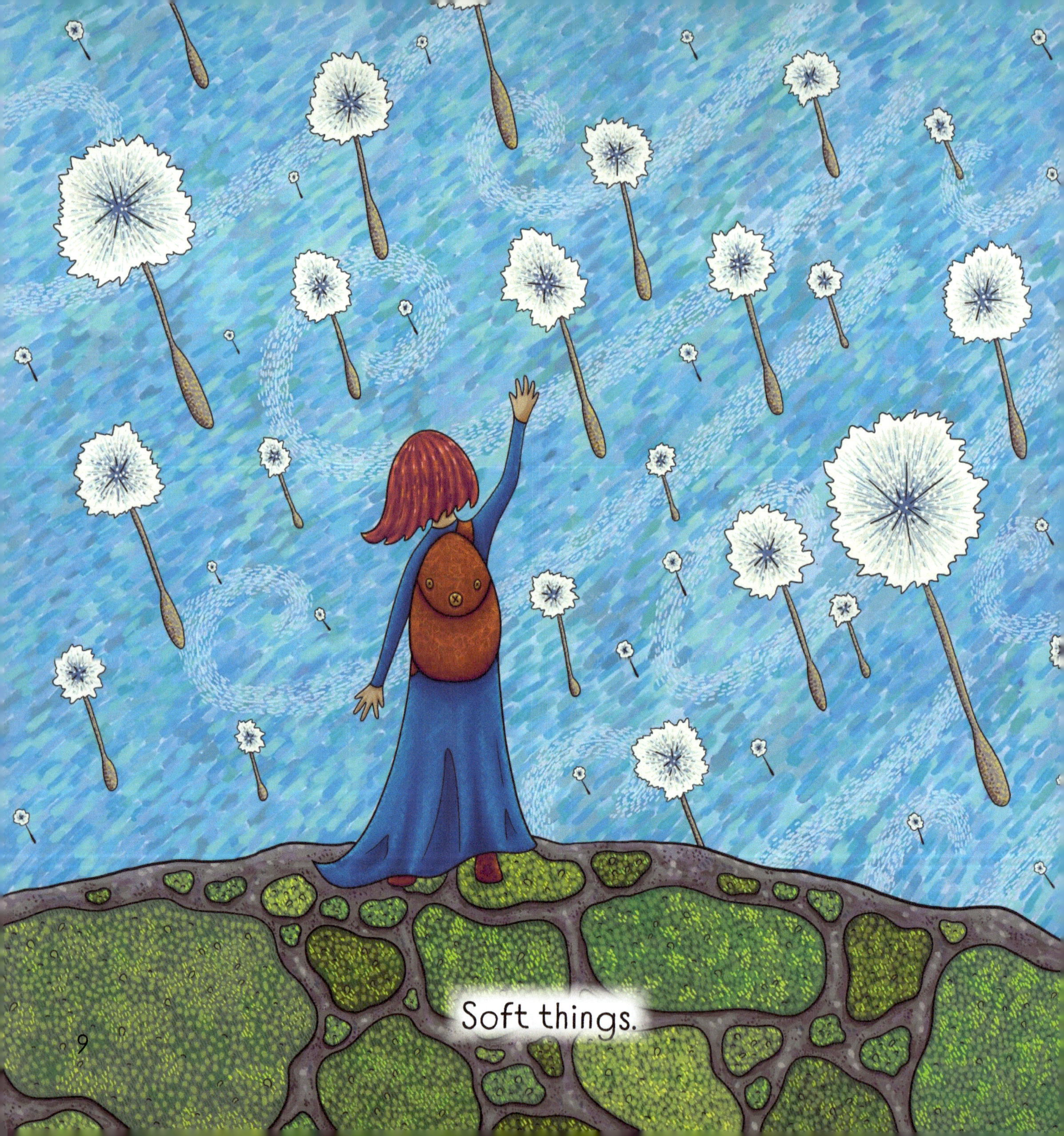

Soft things.

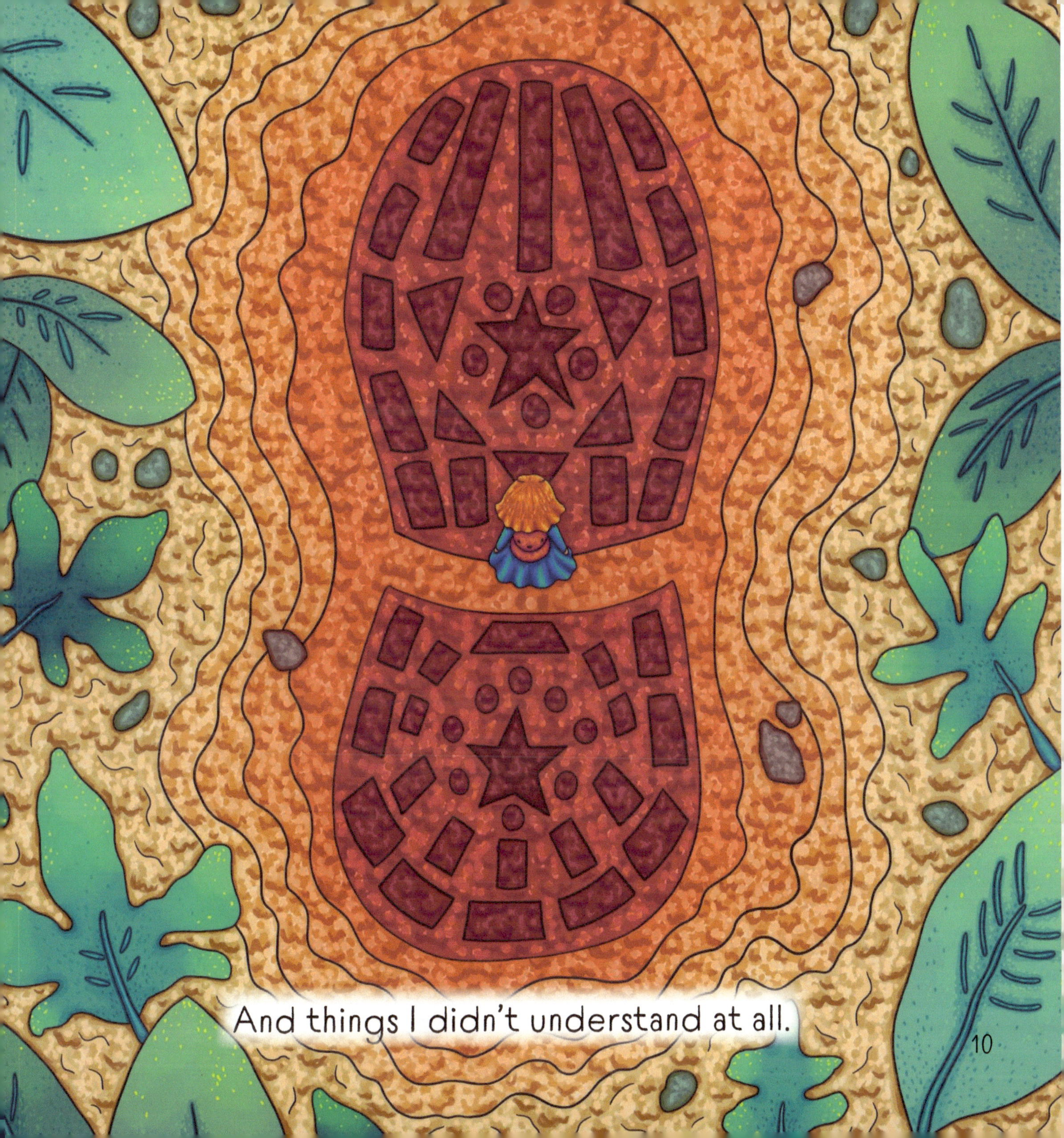

And things I didn't understand at all.

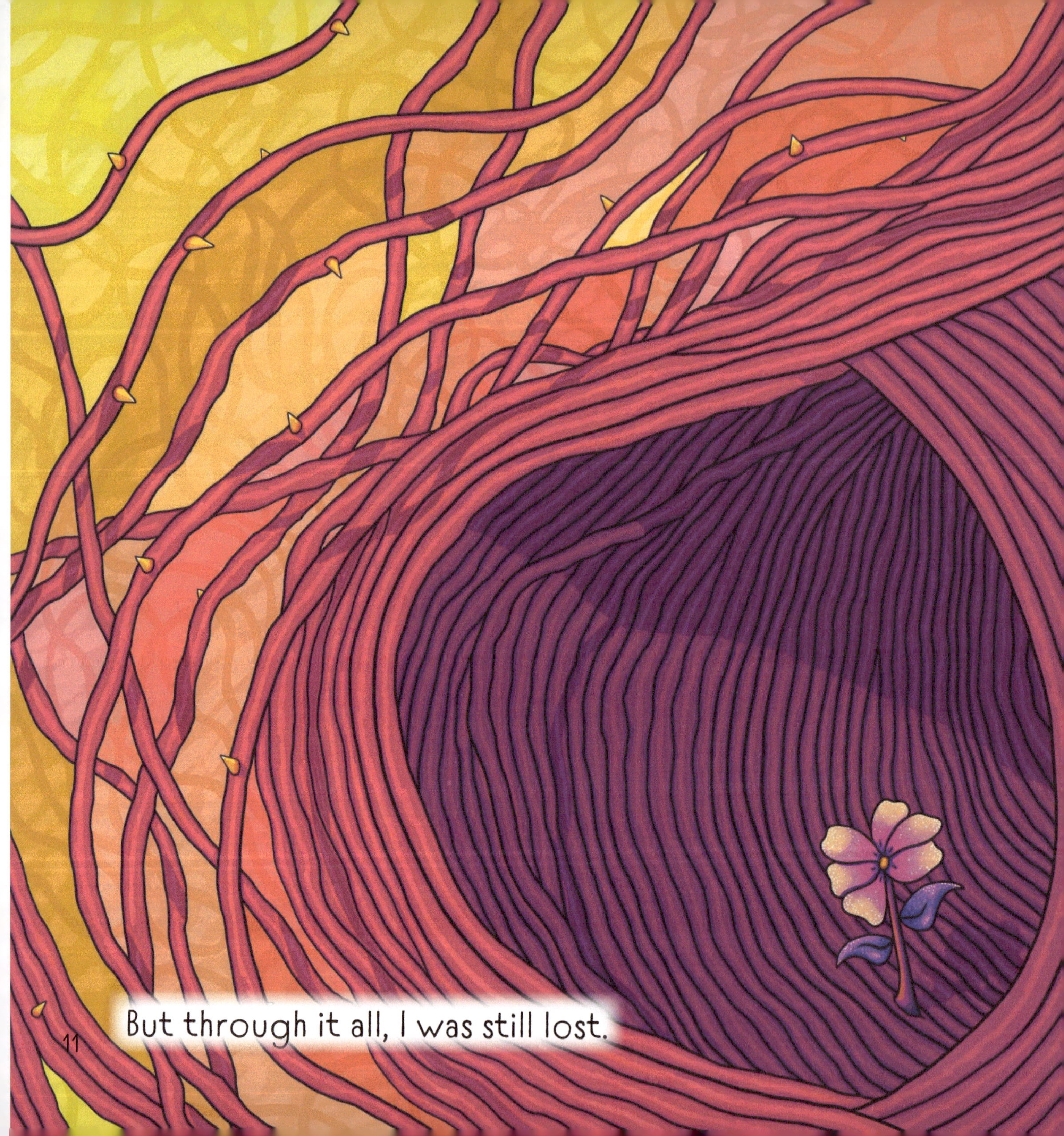
But through it all, I was still lost.

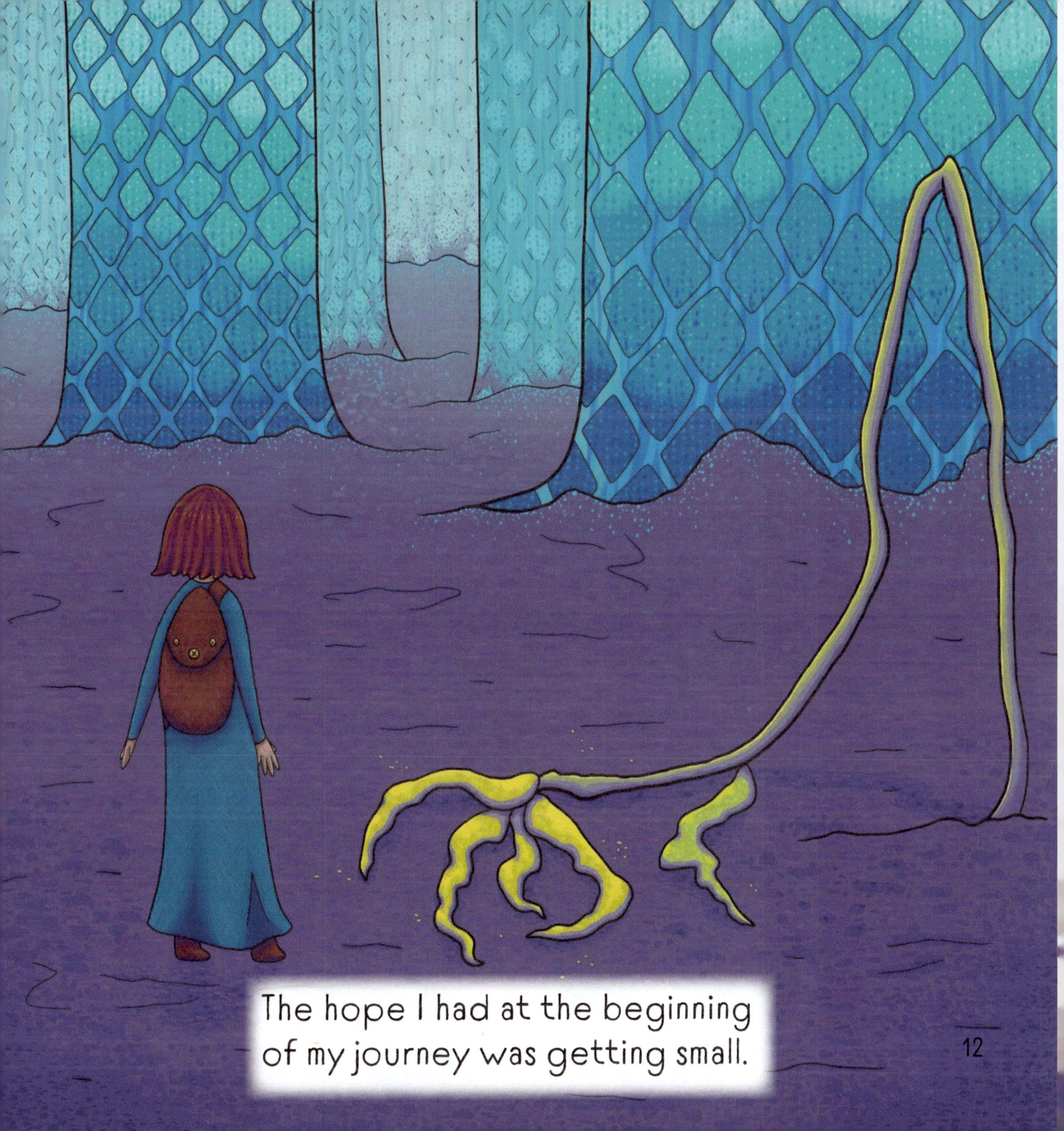

The hope I had at the beginning
of my journey was getting small.

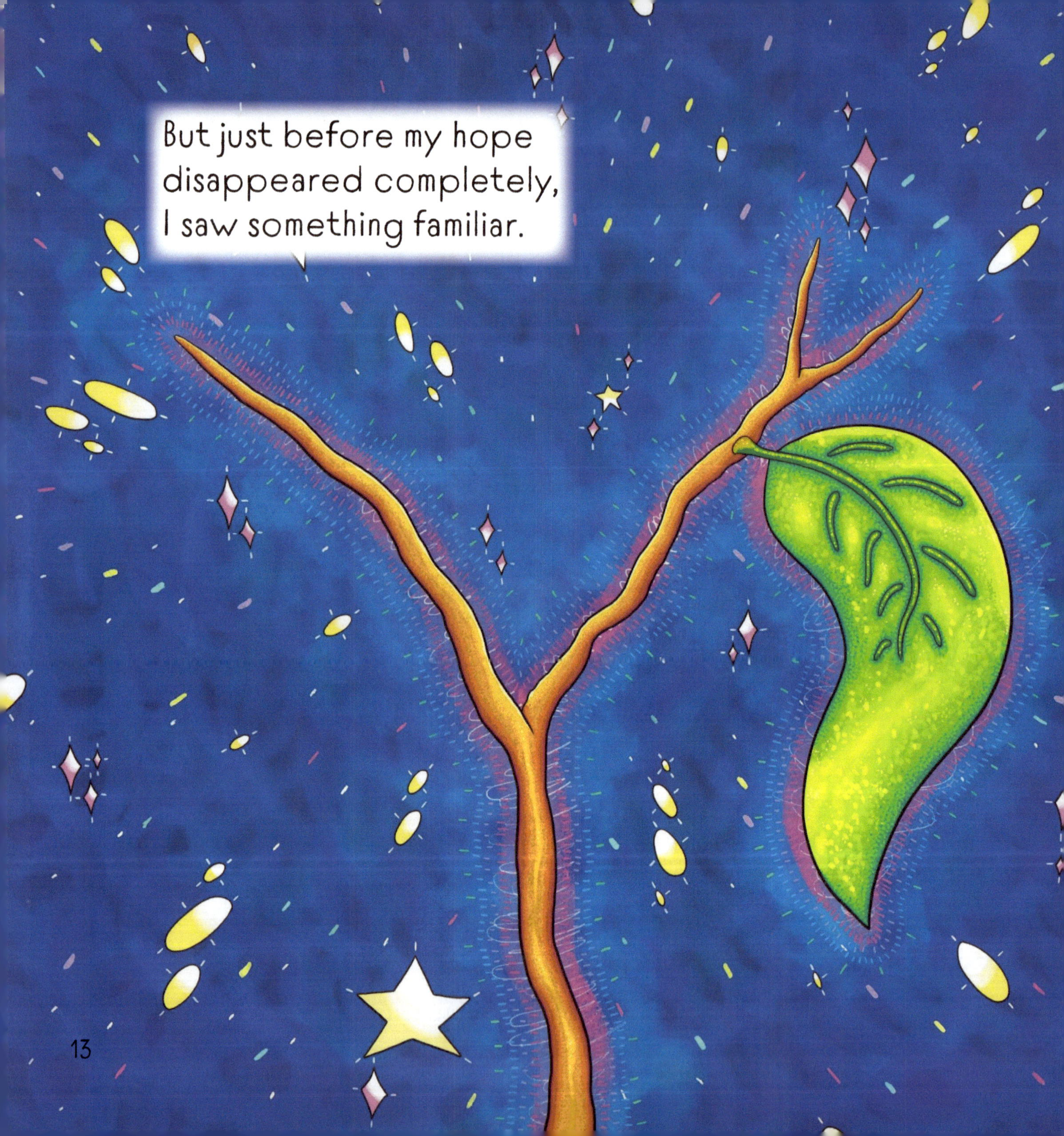
But just before my hope
disappeared completely,
I saw something familiar.

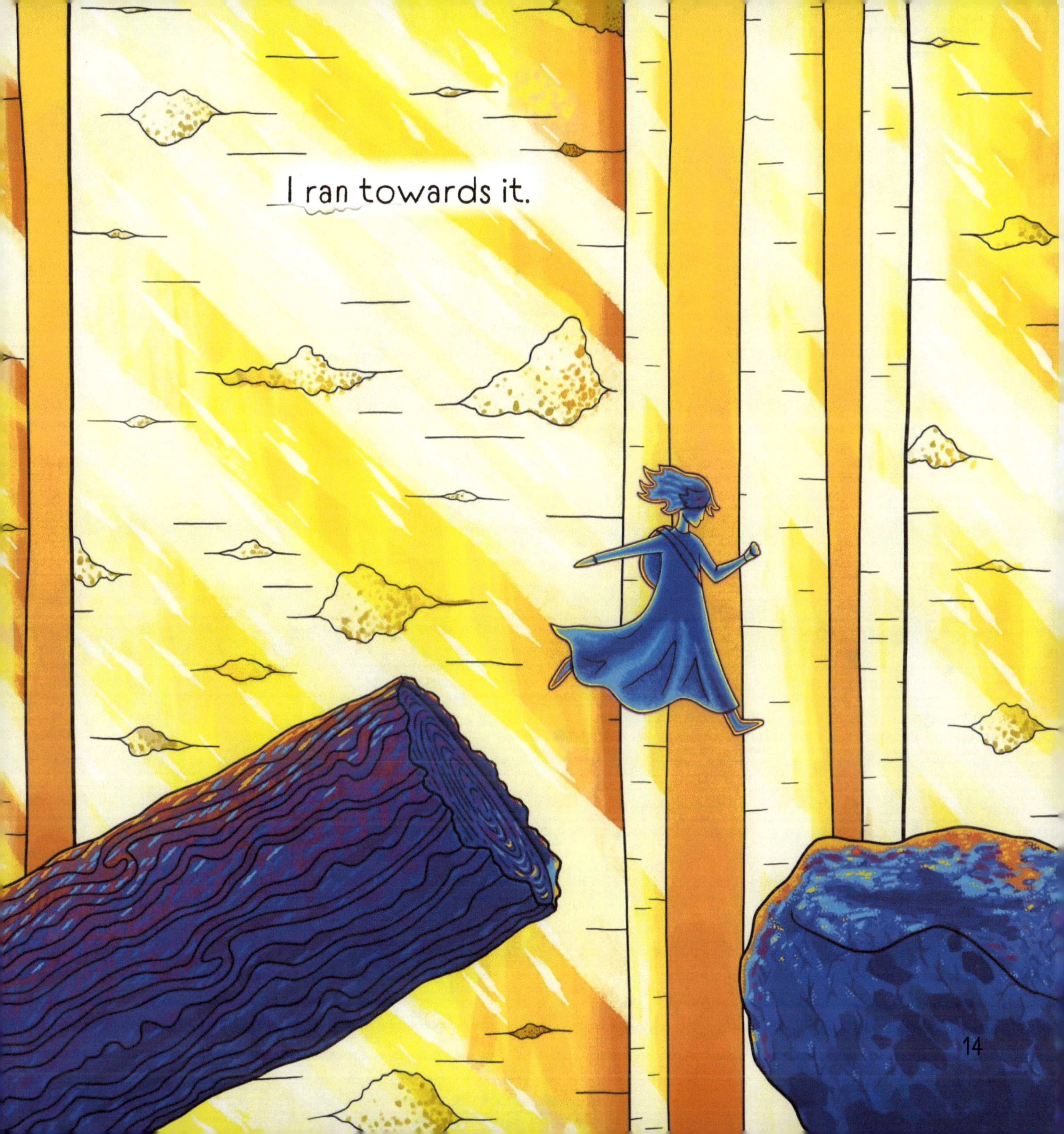
I ran towards it.

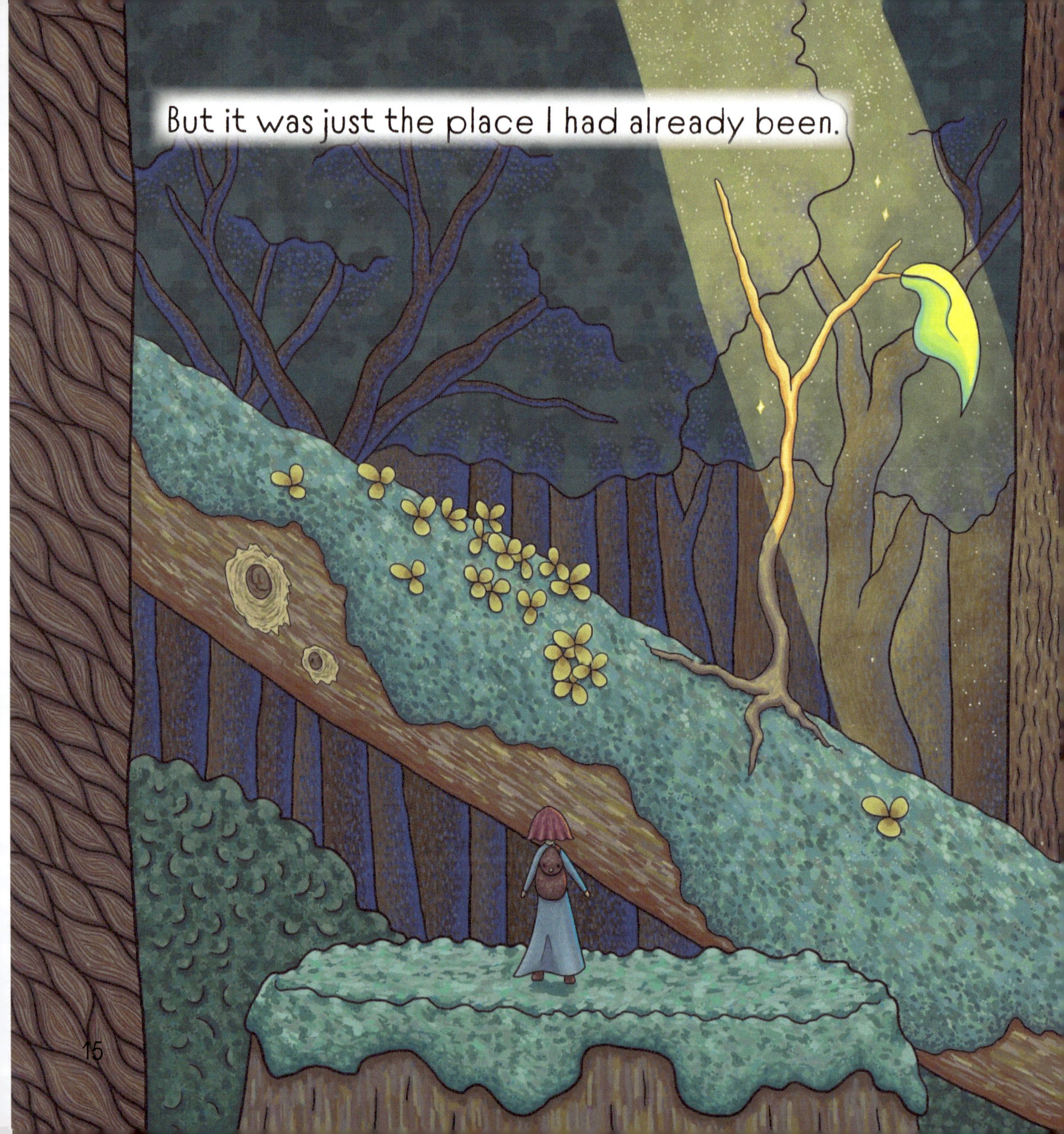

15

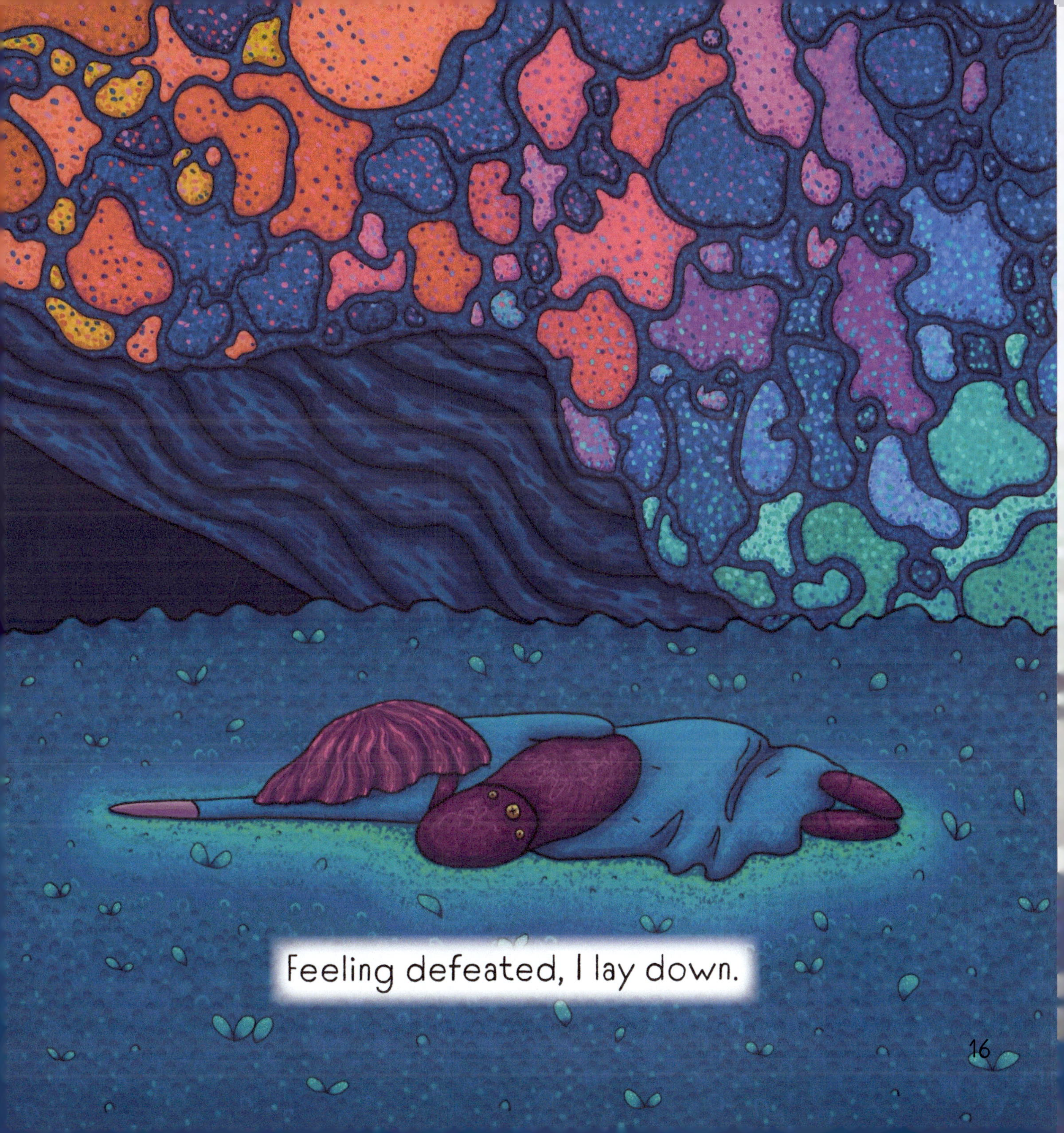

16

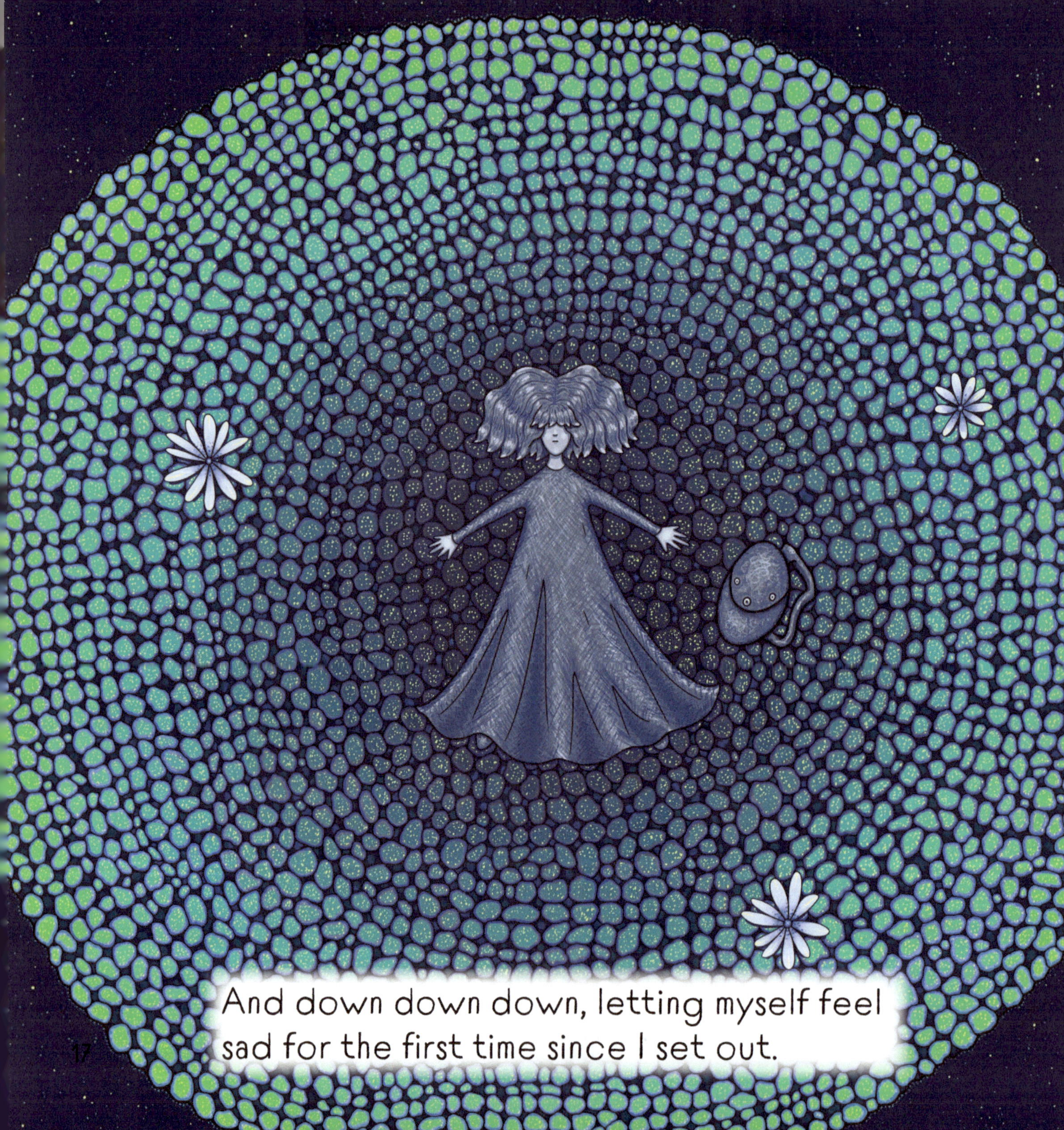

And down down down, letting myself feel
sad for the first time since I set out.

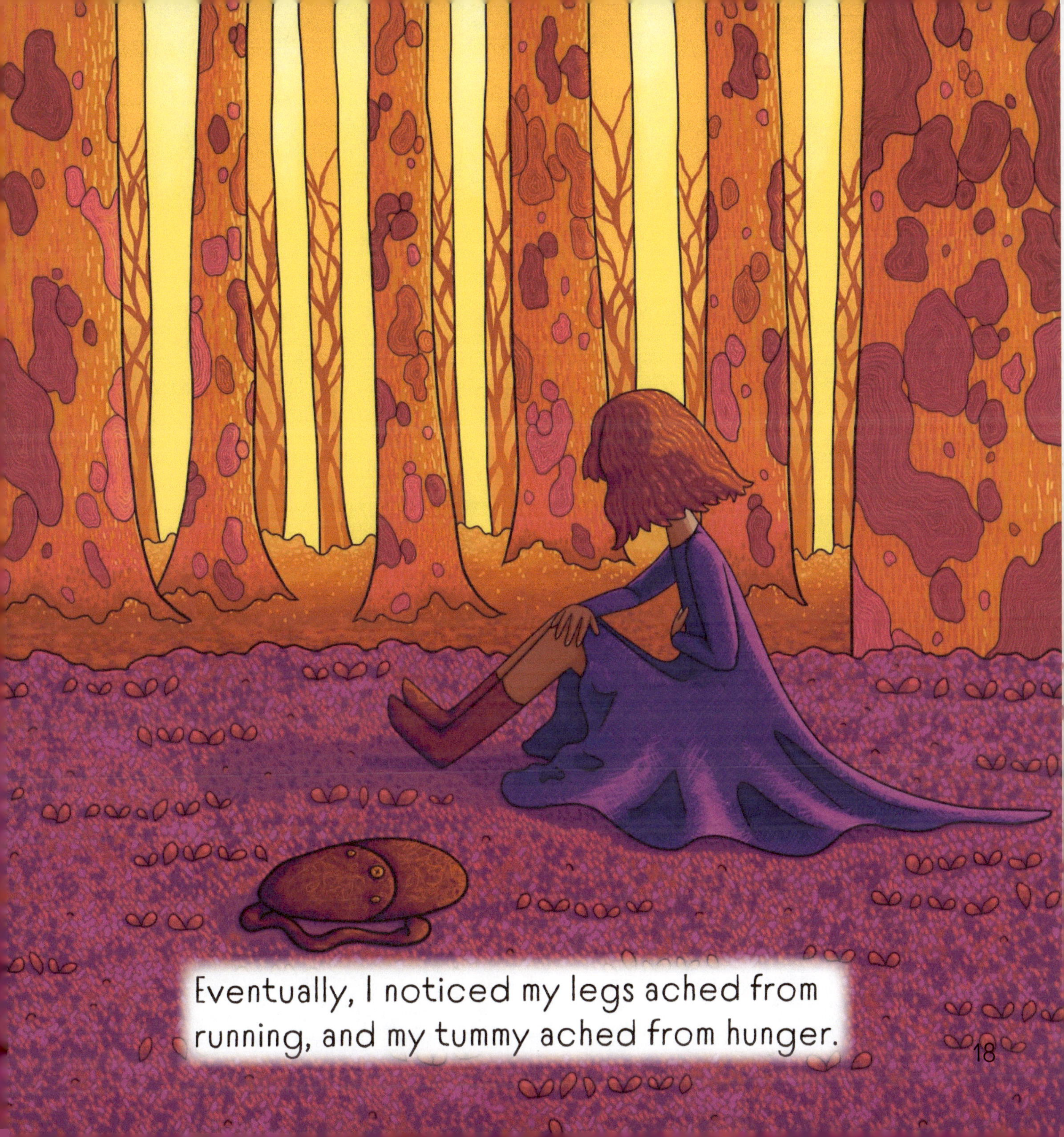
Eventually, I noticed my legs ached from
running, and my tummy ached from hunger.

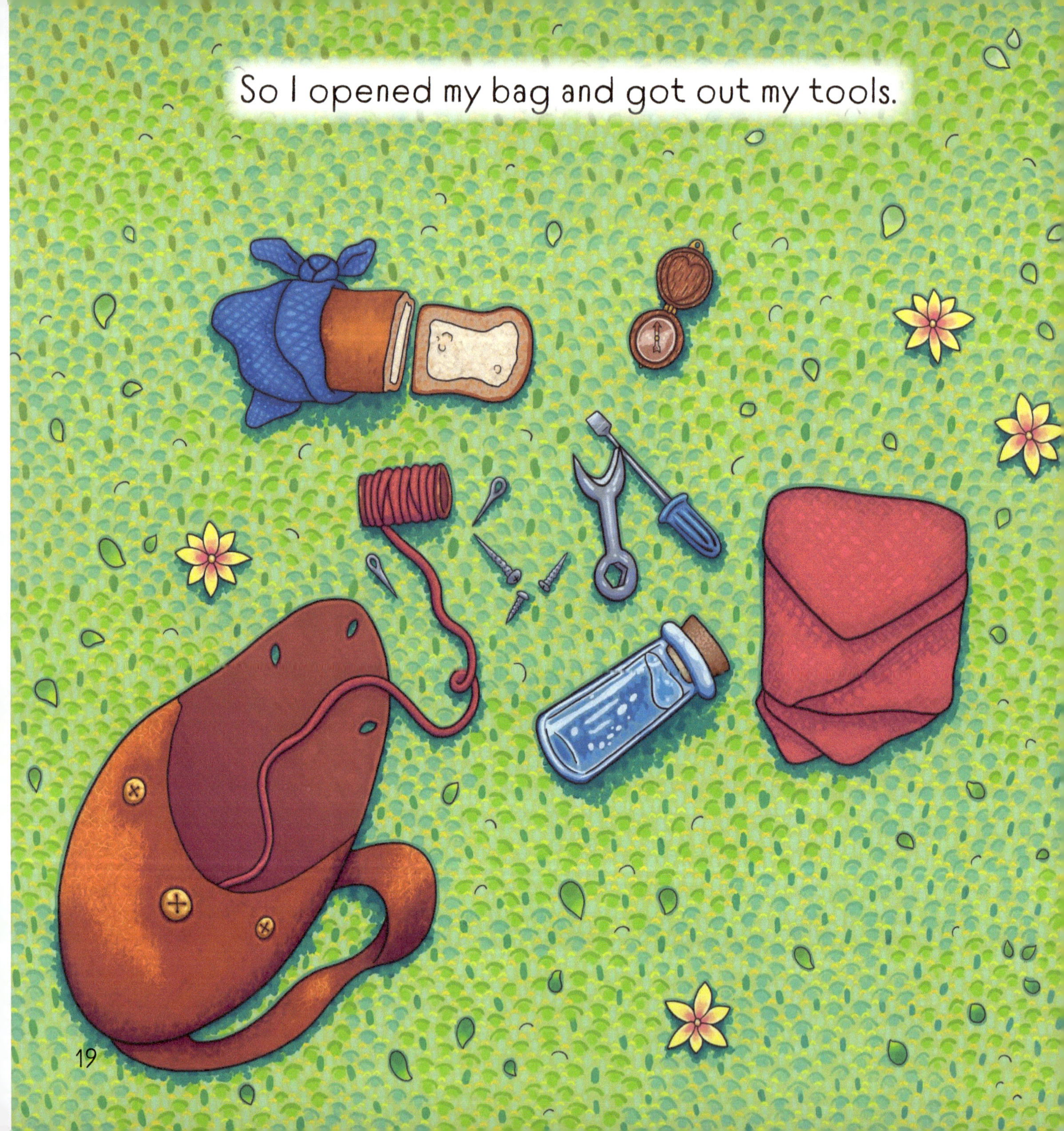
So I opened my bag and got out my tools.

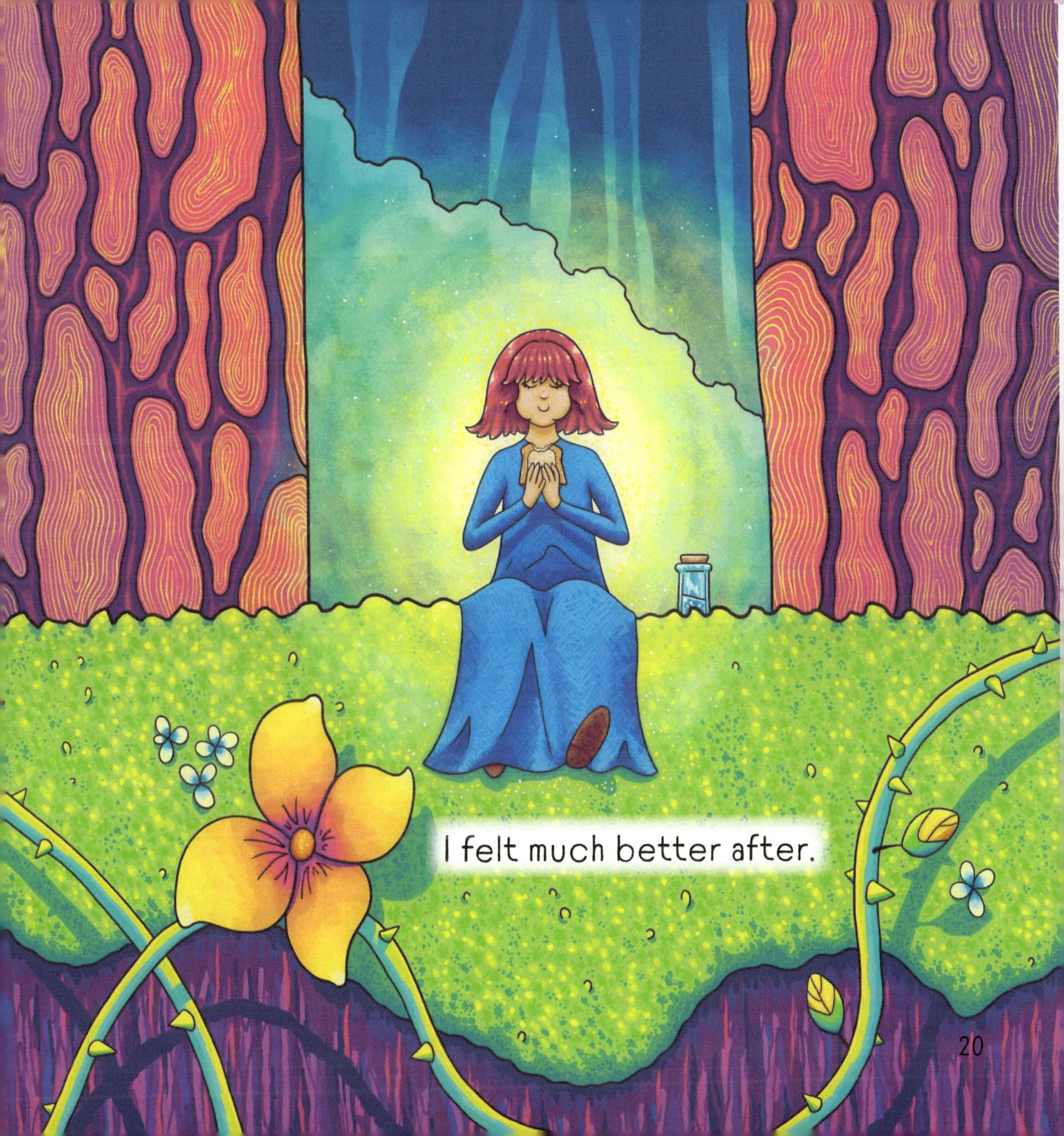

20

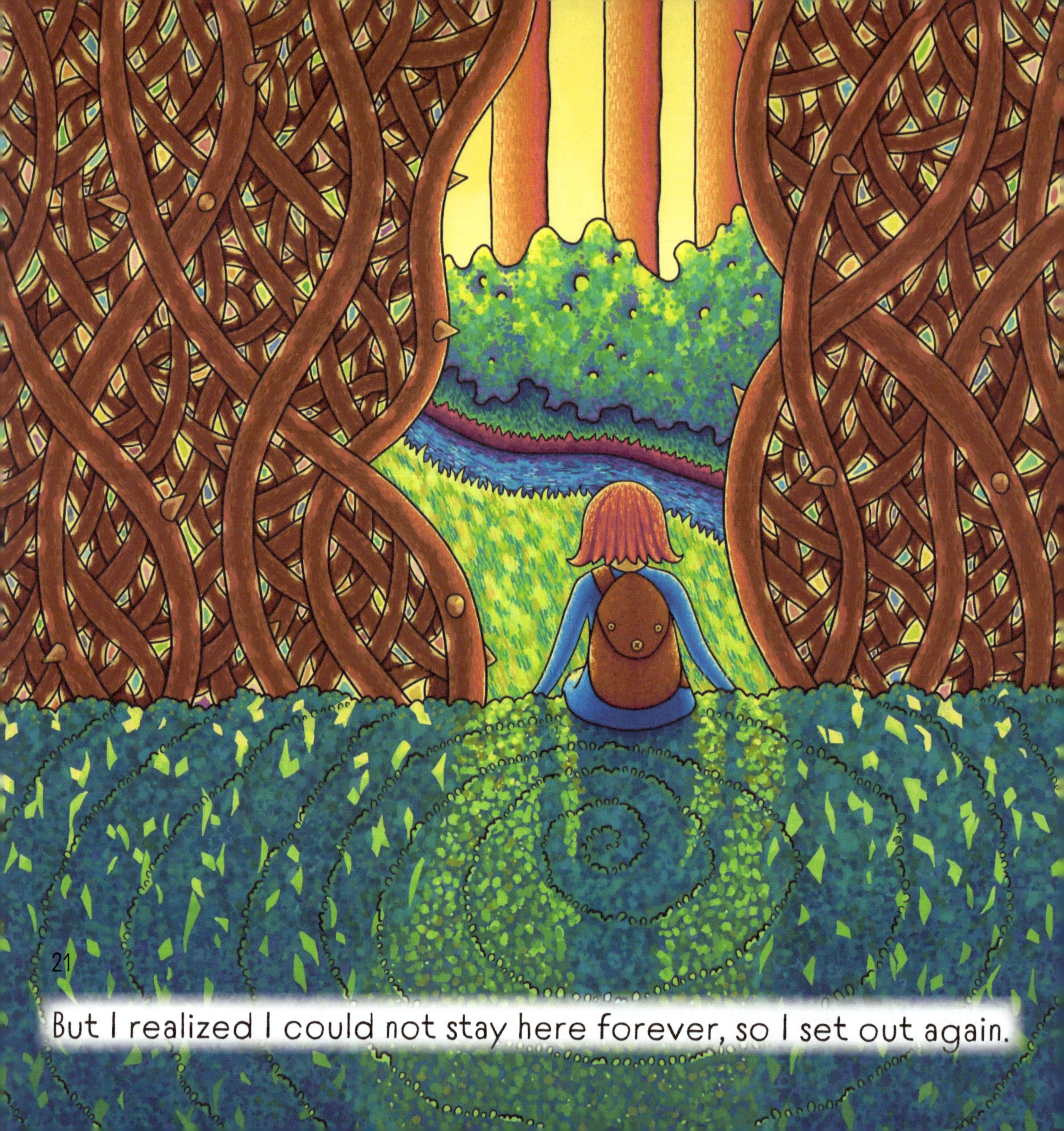

But I realized I could not stay here forever, so I set out again.

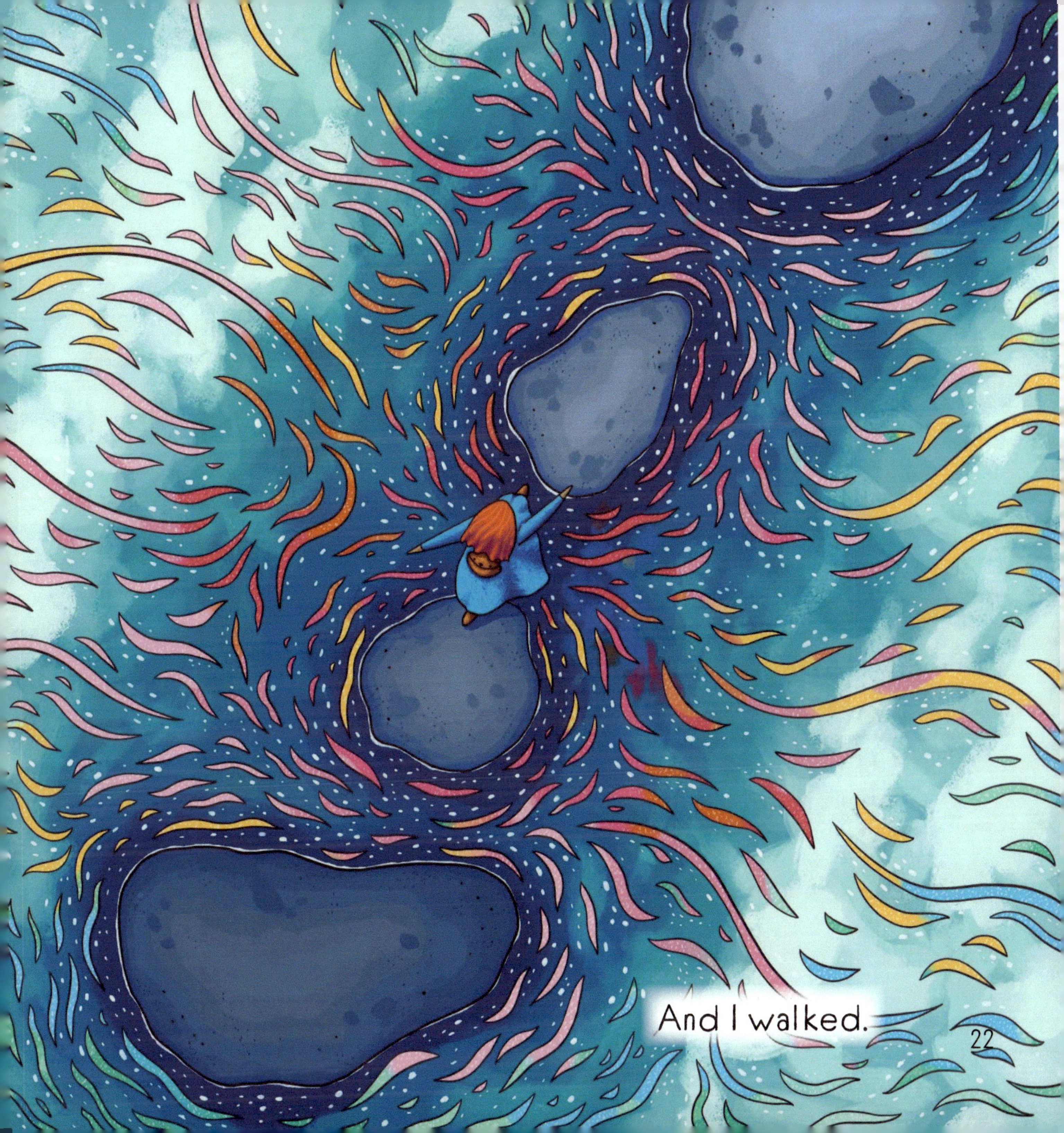
And I walked.
22

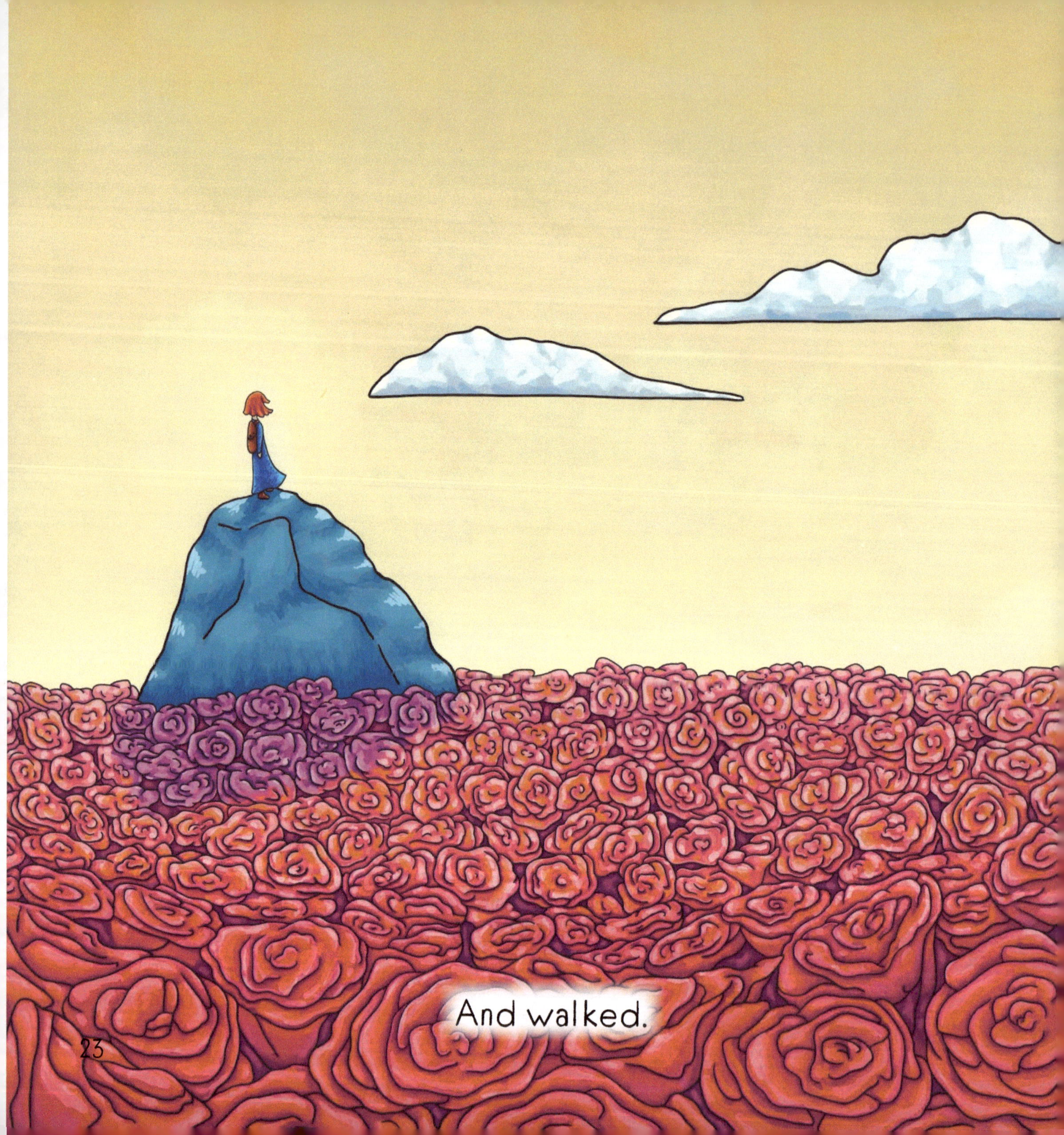
And walked.
23

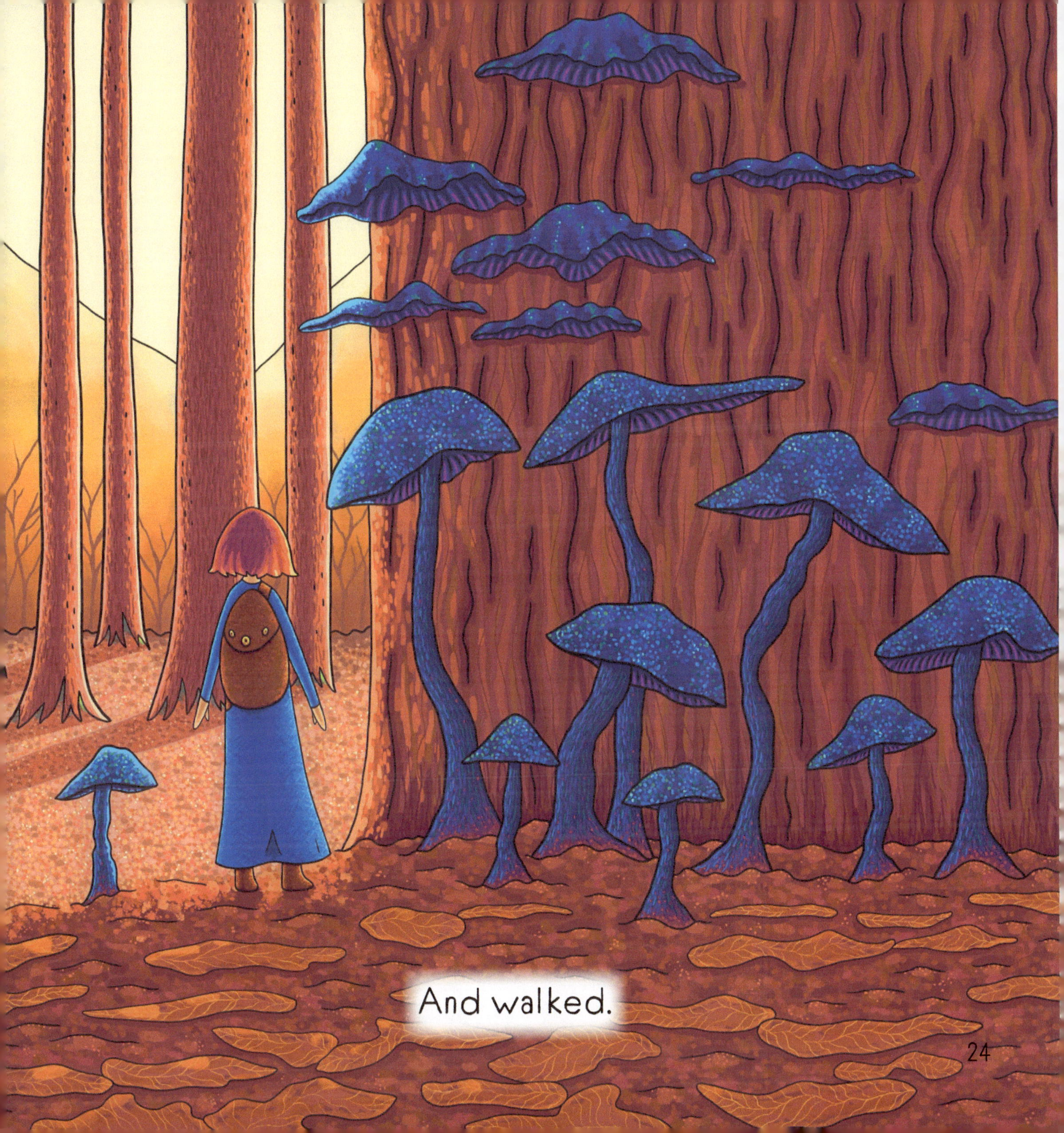
And walked.

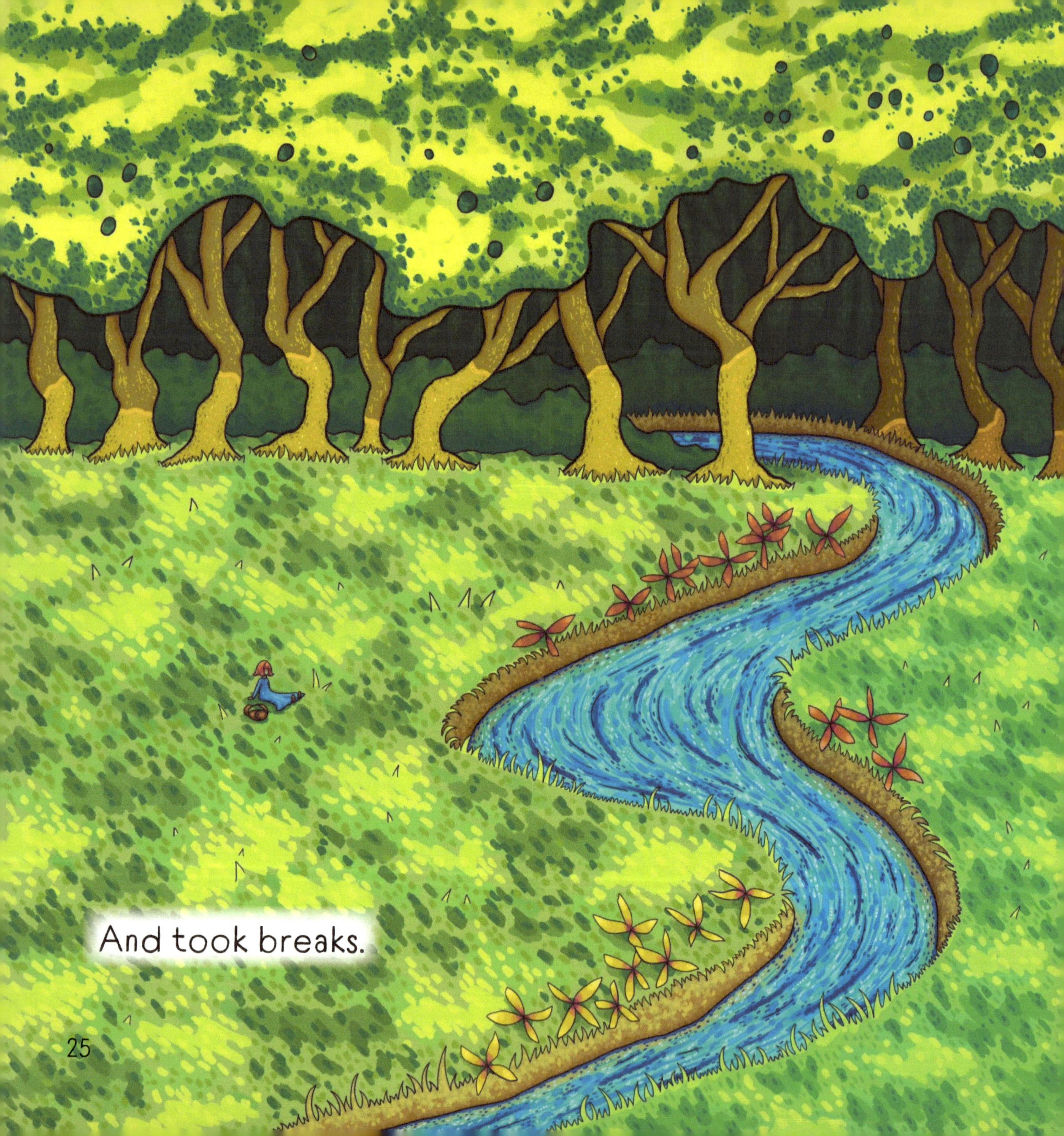

And took breaks.

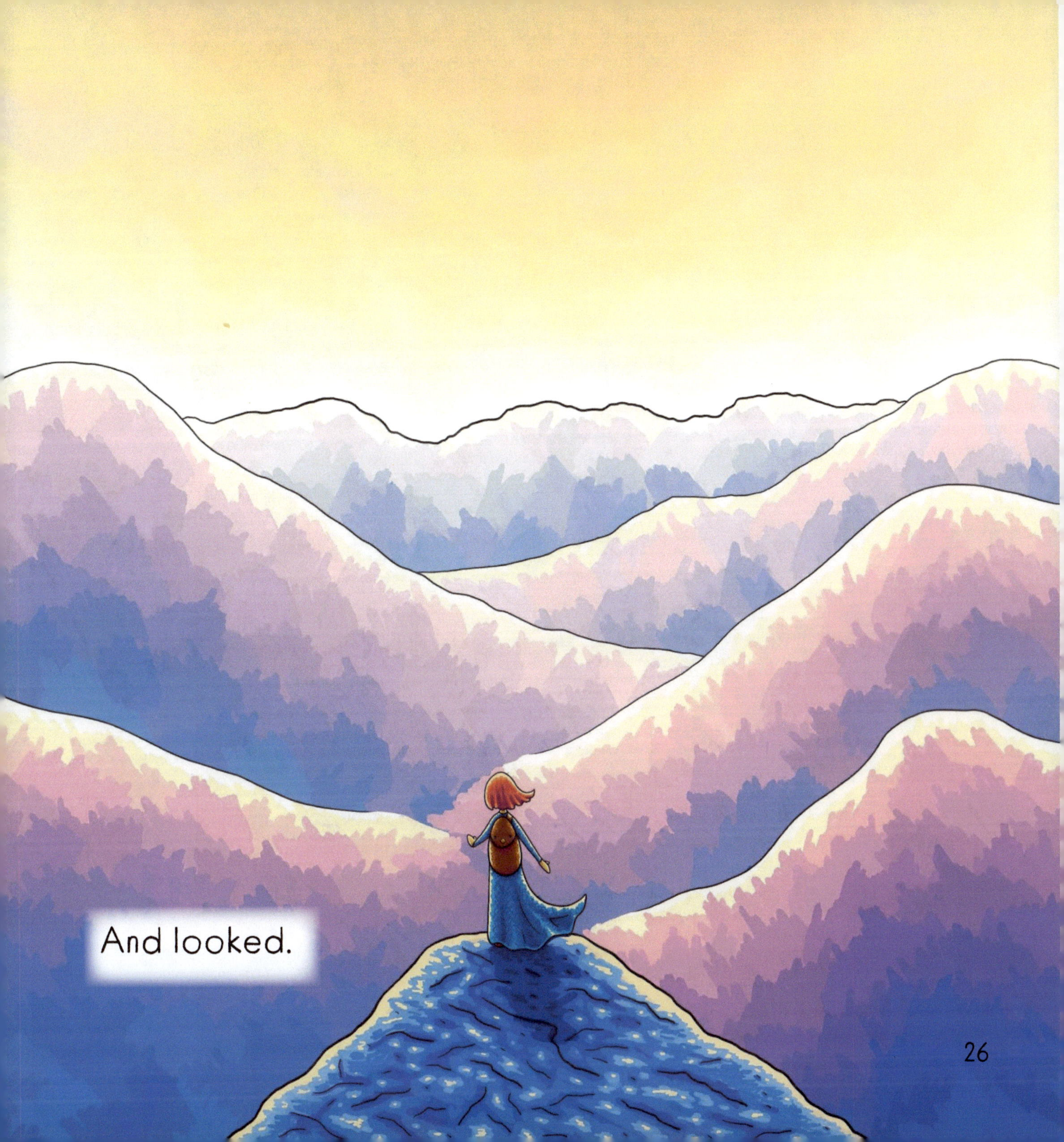

26

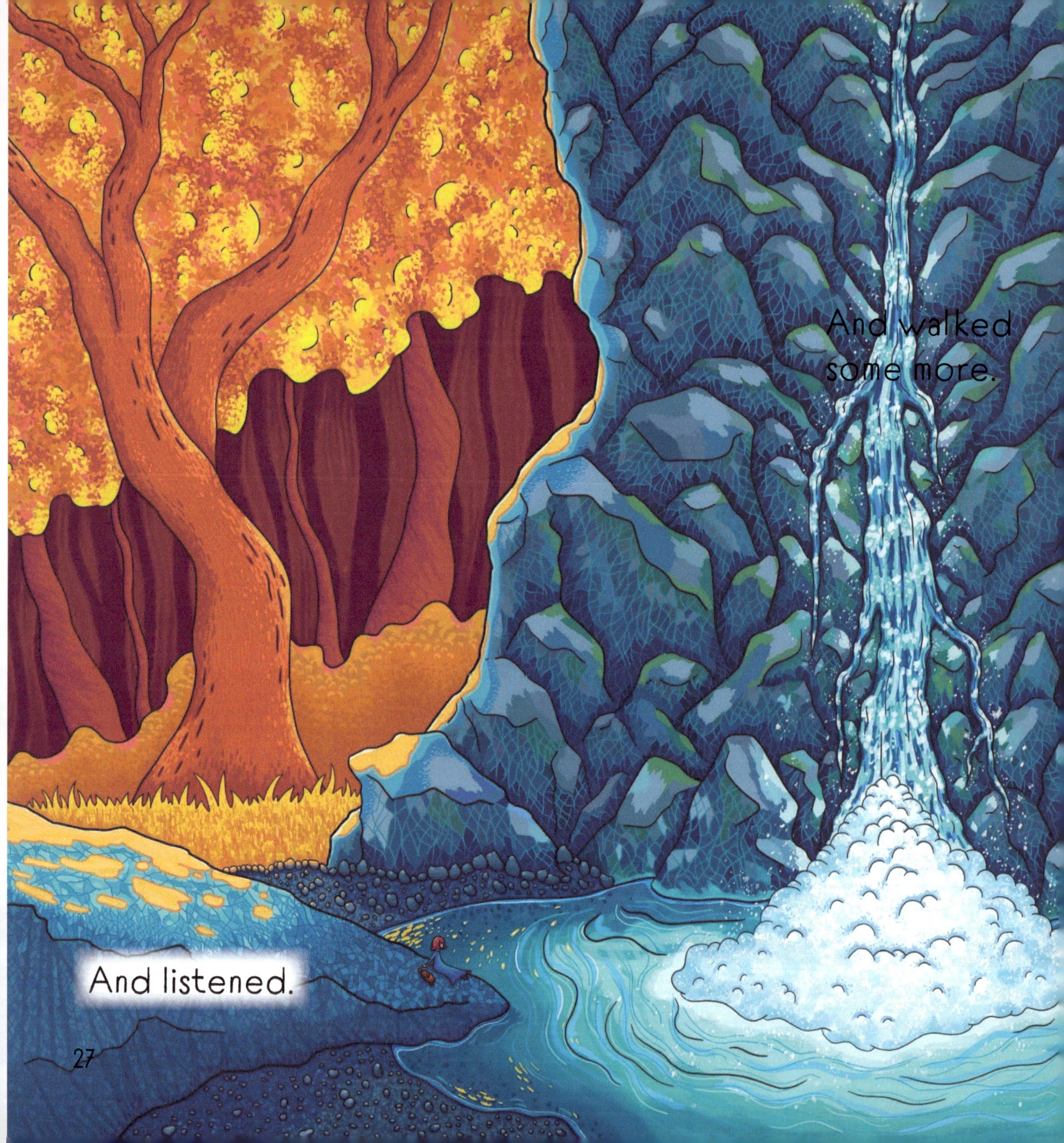
And walked
some more.
And listened.
27

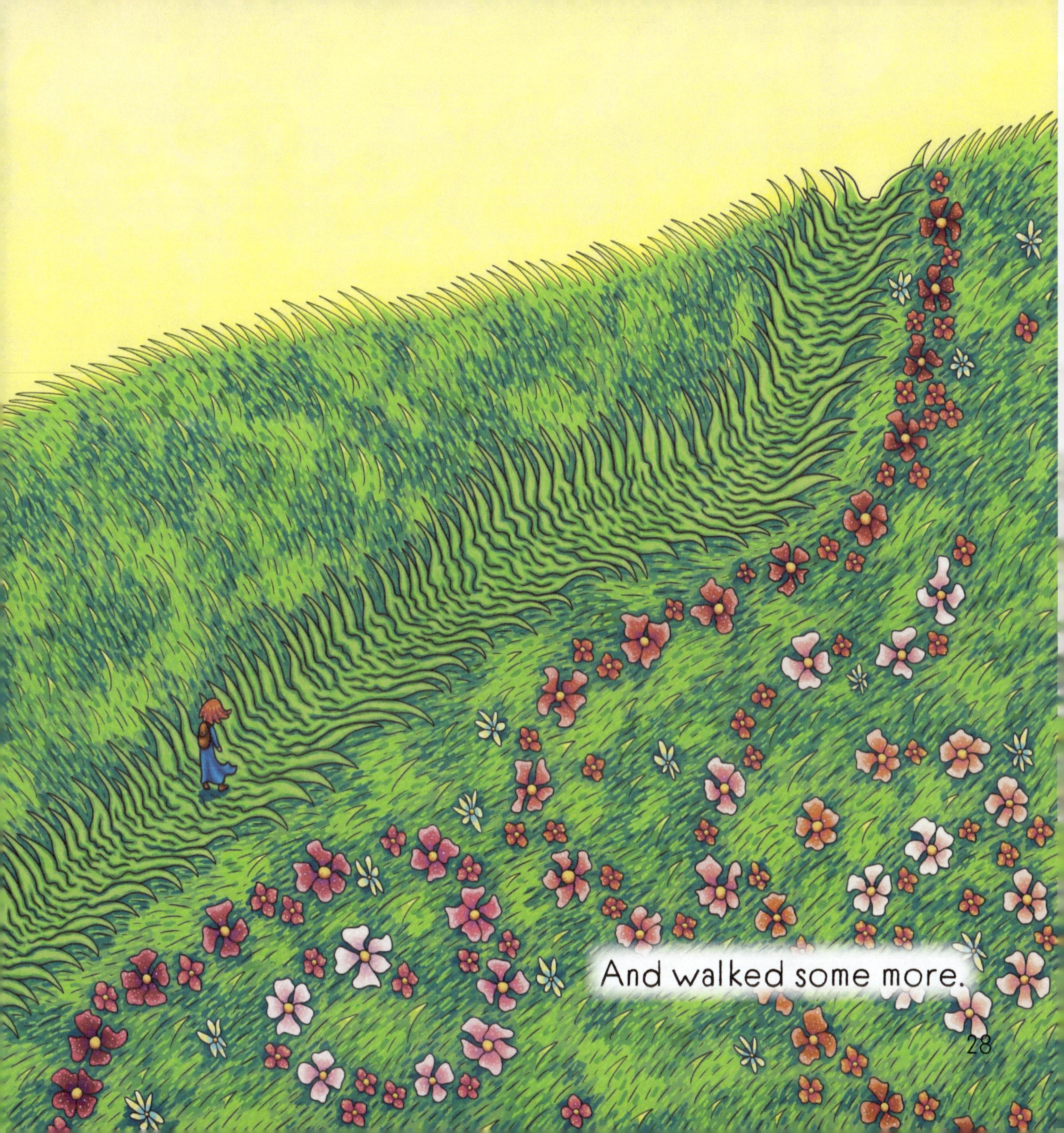

And walked some more.

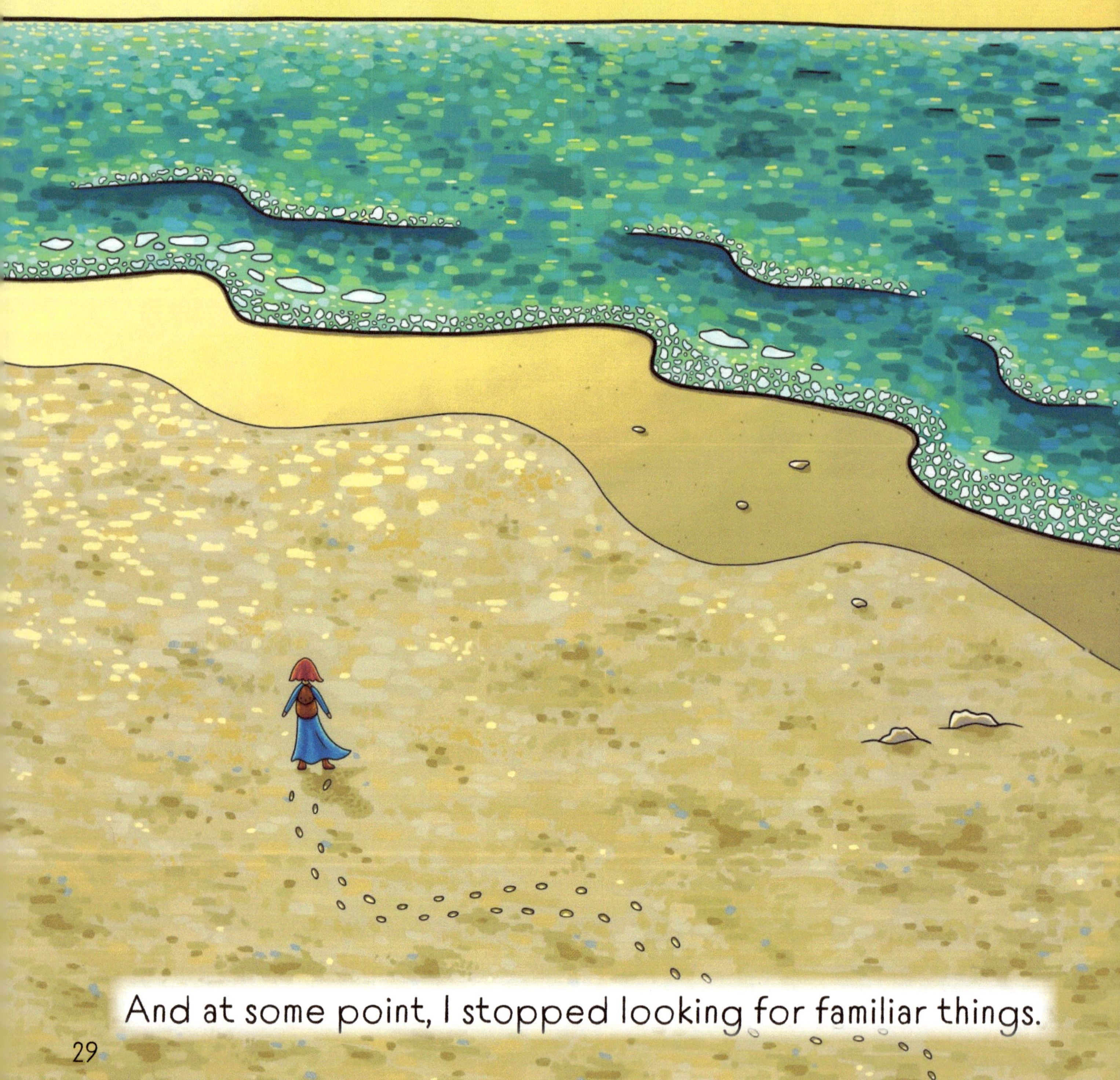

And at some point, I stopped looking for familiar things.

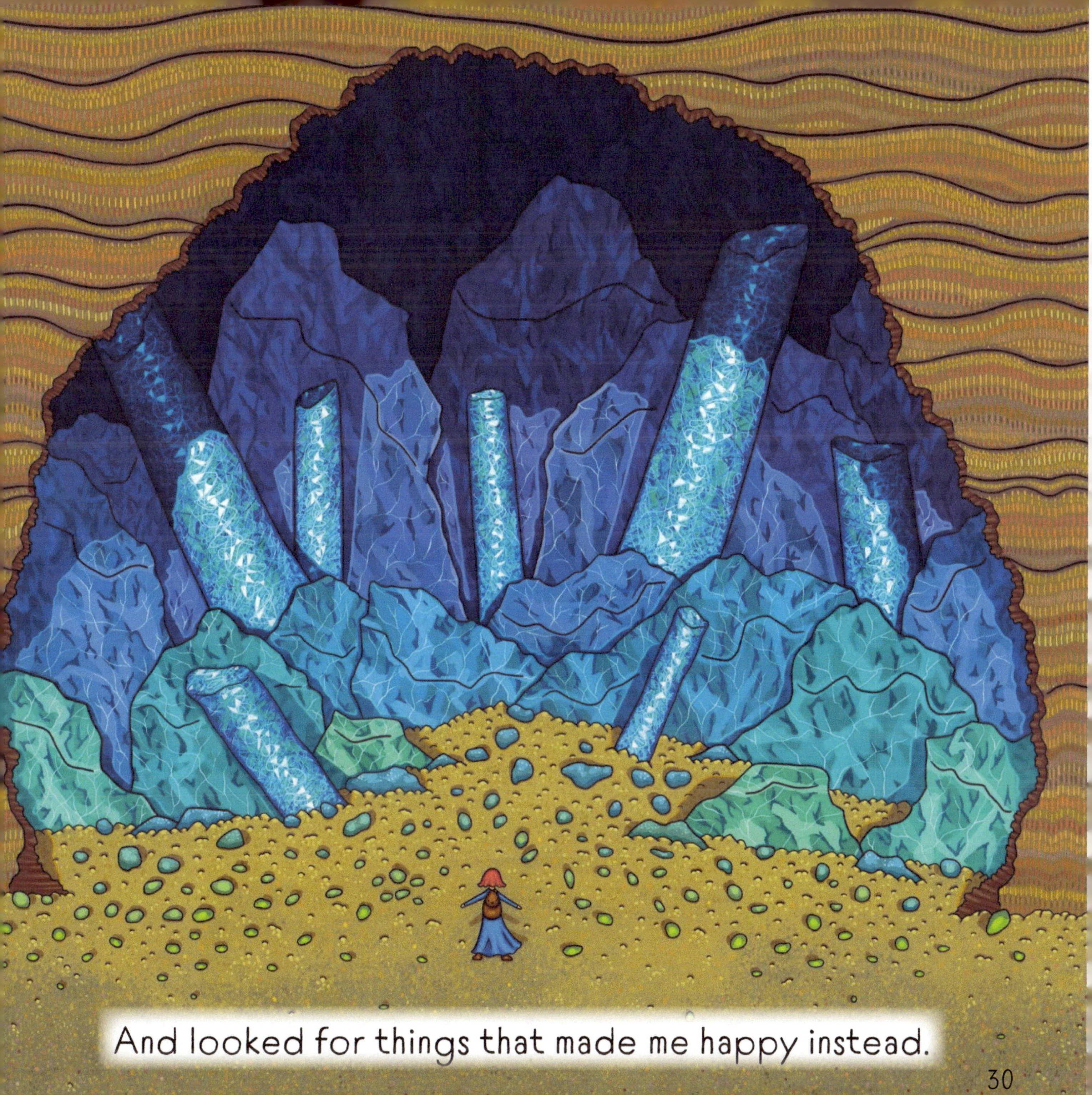

And looked for things that made me happy instead.

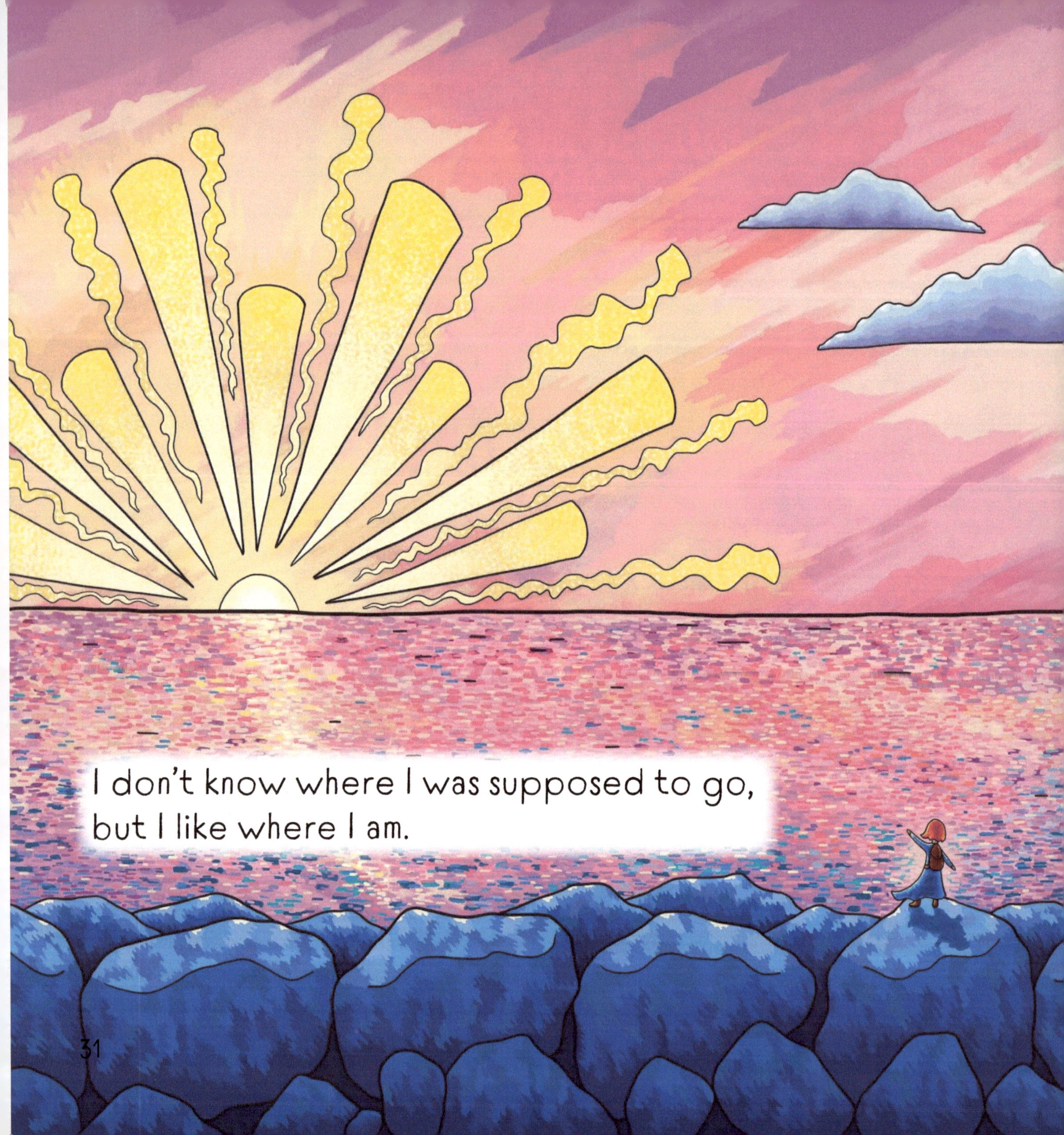

I don't know where I was supposed to go,
but I like where I am.

THE END

AUTHOR NOTE

One of the best things about being little is having so much time to imagine your future. You get to picture your house, the jobs that would be the most fun, the love you will have, and the name of your pet tiger.

So, one of the hardest things about growing up is that you never really stop imagining your future. You could be all grown up in your own place and still think about what corner to put your tiger's bed in. And it will hurt when someone tells you for the first time that it's not legal to own a tiger. It wouldn't be happy in a house anyway. They are too wild and need space to run.

No one's life can turn out exactly how they planned it. And that's upsetting no matter if you are five or fifty. But you can plan to try your best no matter where you end up. You can grieve the life you thought you'd have. You can let it hurt and curl up into a mad, sad little ball. Then you can let it go and find every wonderful thing you can because you will find them.

Love, Anya Blue

www.ingramcontent.com/pod-product-compliance
Lightning Source LLC
Chambersburg PA
CBHW042127030726
47599CB00002B/381